Scarred

Scarred

A Civil War Novel of Redemption

ISBN-13: 9781530379743
ISBN-10: 1530379741
Library of Congress Control Number: 2016903783
CreateSpace Independent Publishing Platform
North Charleston, South Carolina

Prologue

Virginia – 1863

G RAY EARLY MORNING light seeped through the tall sycamores next to the riverbank. The hollow sound of a distant woodpecker broke the silence. The scope of a rifle followed the Confederate sharpshooter as he climbed a tree to his hidden platform. The scope's spider lines centered on the man's head and Zach Harkin squeezed the trigger. Blood and bone splattered against the tree as the gunshot echoed through the forest.

Zach climbed the tree and stared at the dead man whose lower jaw had been blown away. This same sharpshooter had shot his best friend the day before. His upper torso leaned against the tree in a sitting position, both legs splayed out in front of him. His eyes were still open, and Zach felt as if they were looking directly at him with a shocked expression. He searched and found the man's logbook. As he flipped through, he found the last entry from the day before:

Shot a man on the other side of the river. He was on picket duty. Poor bastard. Two more days and I'm on two-week leave to go home. Seems like an eternity since I've seen her.

Then a small picture fell from the pages. Zach stared at the image of the most beautiful woman he had ever seen. He closed the book, slid it into his pocket and climbed down the tree. His thirst for revenge had turned to guilt and the need for redemption.

I

Knoxville, Tennessee –1908

CHRIS MARTIN READ the sign above the door: "Harkin and Son, Gunsmiths." A bell tinkled as he entered. The old man behind the counter had a deep scar from his hairline across his cheek to his chin, but even more noticeable was the scar around his neck, just below the jawbone. A tight necklace was etched in his skin. It looked like it had been made by a rope. The well-worn wood-planked floor creaked as Chris walked to the counter. A steaming pot on an old, potbellied stove in a back corner of the room reminded him of the way his grandfather made coffee, just boiling the grounds in water. The fresh morning air mixed with the pungent smell of Hoppe's gun oil that permeated the room. The sun shone through the front windows, illuminating the man's face and casting a sharp shadow over the rifles hanging on the wall behind him.

He introduced himself and offered the old man his hand.

"Zach Harkin. Welcome. And how can I help you?"

"I'm a columnist with *The New York World*." Harkin's face turned dour, but Chris continued. "My paper has asked me to write a series of articles about the Civil War, and specifically about your exploits at Shiloh as a sharpshooter. Your heroism is well known. Is that coffee I smell?"

"Mr. Martin, I don't care much for reporters and what I did at Shiloh could have been accomplished by anybody handy with a rifle. I am no 'hero' and have never claimed to be one. I do not think further conversation would do you any good."

Looking for another tack, Chris said, "You sure have a lot of handsome firearms here. Mind if I look around a bit?"

"As you wish."

When *The World* gave this assignment to Chris, he decided the first thing to do was to learn about guns: how they were used, their various advantages and disadvantages, their power, range, accuracy, and ease of action. He'd visited several gunsmiths in the New York area, discussing the attributes of Spencers, Sharps, Colts, Remingtons, and all the variations. The gunsmiths were eager to talk about their wares, and surprisingly, he developed a keen interest himself.

Chris spent several days consulting with John Jovino, a noted gun expert in New York City. Jovino had heard of Zach Harkin, and even knew of his gun shop in Knoxville. Jovino had been able to guess about some of the rifles Zach might have, and prepared Chris with details.

Chris picked up a beautifully restored 1861 model Springfield rifle. While it appeared to have been heavily used, the stock had been refinished and the metal parts buffed to a steely shine. He looked down the barrel, noting the rifling. "Nice 1861 model," he said. "First Springfield that had rifling, wasn't it?"

"Yep," the old man said, not looking up. Zach's big hands dwarfed the small pencil he was using, but the writing was neat and concise. His sleeves were rolled up just below his elbows, revealing large forearms covered in small scars. Both wrists bore identical scars that looked like thin bracelets, probably also caused by ropes. Chris thought to himself that this man must have seen the worst of the war.

He picked up a Model 1855 Colt revolving rifle. Its six-shot cylinder, designed to rotate each time the gun fired, made it essentially a repeating rifle. The problem was that sometimes two cartridges exploded, one going down the barrel and the other through the shooter's hand.

"I wonder if the original owner has a bullet hole in his hand," Chris said.

The old man looked up, mildly interested.

Under the glassed-topped counter, another rifle caught Chris's eye. It was a Whitmore forty-two caliber breechloader, and it appeared to be in mint condition. "Mind if I have a closer look?" Chris asked.

The man handed the rifle over slowly, as if it was something very special.

"Hmmm, a Nathaniel Whitmore. Made in Boston, probably 1855 or so," Chris said. "Looks like it has never been fired."

The old man stopped writing and looked up. Chris was finally getting his attention.

"This lollipop rear sight sure made it effective for long-range shooting. Should be accurate way north of five or six hundred yards. Correct me if I'm wrong but this rifle was one of the favorites used by Berdan's Sharpshooters in the war." Chris knew Zach had served with Berdan, and hoped he would be impressed.

"I have to admit, you know your guns," he said. "I guess there is no harm in having some coffee."

Chris turned away slightly to avoid showing his smile.

They sat down on wooden chairs on either side of the stove. The room was quiet, except for an old clock ticking somewhere in the next room. The old man looked troubled. Between sips of coffee, he studied the floor with a deep frown. His hair was gray, as was his beard, and the scar down the side of his face looked like lightning streaking between them. He was in excess of six feet tall, trim, and his clothing was timeworn but neat and clean. He wore a pair of bib overalls with various tools sticking out of the pockets.

He looked up at Chris as if to speak, then hesitated, and returned his gaze to the floor. Chris stayed quiet.

The old man got up, walked behind the counter, and started wiping down the glass.

Chris started toward the door. "Mind if I come back tomorrow?"

"I'm here every day except Sundays," he said flatly.

The Harkin shop was located on Gay Street in downtown Knoxville. Chris knew Zach's father had moved there from Manchester, Vermont in the 1850s. Knoxville was a bustling "new South" city, having grown steadily since the end of the war. Gay Street was lined with brick buildings housing stores, shops, and offices. The streets were also brick, with two sets of electric streetcar tracks connecting the city to outlying areas. The light posts lining the street had dozens of wires strung from their cross members, reinforcing the impression of vibrancy and growth. The concrete sidewalks were crowded with shoppers and businessmen.

Two men loaded newspaper bundles onto a covered wagon with "*The Knoxville Sentinel*" painted in red on the sides, and workers put the finishing touches on the soon-to-open Bijou Theater directly across the street. A few motor carriages passed by, the smell of their black exhaust mixed with the strong odor of horse urine.

At the Lamar Hotel, a cheerful older man behind the reception desk looked up as Chris entered, a nametag pinned to his shirt said, "Jerome Daniels."

"Mister Martin?" he asked.

"How would you know that?" Chris asked, surprised.

The man laughed and said he could tell from the cut of Chris's suit jacket, and they had only one reservation from New York. The bald clerk wore a white cotton shirt, wrinkled and stained in front. His footsteps sounded strange as he came out from behind the desk, and Chris couldn't avoid glancing down at his wooden leg.

"Chattanooga Campaign, back in sixty-three. Rebel cannonball. This is my sixth stub," he said, matter of factly. "Wear 'em out almost as fast as they can make 'em." He picked up Chris's bag and hobbled toward the staircase.

The wooden leg was rounded on the end, and whenever he took a step, the thump on the old oak floor sounded like the slow cadence of a tired company of soldiers at the end of a long day's march. Going up the stairs, he could only take one step at a time. He led with his good foot, lifted the bag up, and followed with his peg leg, talking all the while. Chris thought it best not to offer a hand. The man seemed too proud to accept his help.

It took a while, but they eventually made it to Chris's third floor room.

As the man unlocked the door, he asked Chris what brought him to Knoxville, and Chris explained that he was interviewing Zach Harkin for a piece to be printed in *The New York World*. When Harkin's name was mentioned, the old man's eyes lit up.

"Do you know him?" Chris asked.

"Went to school with him, hunted and fished with him. We were even at Shiloh together. Yes, you could say I know him."

He said everybody west of the Appalachians knew Zach Harkin, and proceeded to tell about the statue they had wanted to erect near Fountain City Park in his honor. Harkin had fought the idea, threatening to sue the city if they continued their plans, so the idea was eventually dropped.

Jerome placed the bag on a stand while Chris opened the window to let some air into the stuffy room. The counterweights rattled and the screech of a braking streetcar below filled the room. A stiff breeze wafted the heavy blue velvet drapes and they tugged against their gold-colored tiebacks. The floor was the same oak as in the lobby, but had seen much less wear. It was covered with a thin layer of dust, which blew in the breeze. Against the back wall stood a four-poster bed with a mattress that sagged in the middle. A chamber pot sat on a dresser beside a pitcher of water. A vase containing three daisies, all drooping in different directions, sat next to the pitcher.

Chris tipped Jerome, then sat at a small table and wrote a telegram to his editors confirming his arrival and promising his first installment of the Harkin story within a few days. He did not know if he would be able to keep that promise, but he knew his paper was anxious to get started.

He reached into his case and pulled out a framed picture of the woman he hoped to marry, Sarah Elliot. It had been taken with a Kodak Brownie he had purchased shortly before he left. He leaned back in the chair and studied it .The picture was not posed; rather it showed her reading an issue of *The World*. Her eyes were dark and her curly hair hung over her shoulders. Her bangs were wrapped in a lacy headband. He loved the way the image connected their lives.

She shared Chris's excitement about his assignment, and both thought the articles could act as a springboard for his career. They believed the country was hungry for stories about soldiers who had distinguished themselves in the war.

Chris, having been born in 1870, represented the first generation that had not experienced the war. His peers wanted to know more about the men who fought, and how they reintegrated after they came home. *The World* and other newspapers had been relatively silent about the Civil War over the last few decades, and Chris thought it was time to change that.

2

Knoxville, Tennessee—1908

AFTER THE *New York World* reporter left, Zach had decided to close the shop for the day.

The reporter had been nice enough. As a matter of fact, he liked him. He seemed to know an awful lot about guns for a city fellow. Maybe he had just been trying to win Zach over, like any good reporter. If so, he had succeeded. He seemed genuinely interested in what had happened way back then.

A vague darkness followed him as he closed up shop. It was always there, coming closer, then fading. Sometimes it enveloped him and held him captive and he wondered why he was put on this earth.

He went up to his bedroom and sat on the bed. Reaching into the bed stand drawer, he pulled out the logbook he had taken from the dead soldier's side so long ago and stared at the photograph inside. It was an old tintype, but to Zach, the image never lost its freshness and luster. She remained forever beautiful. He ran the back of his index finger slowly over the image. Tears came to his eyes.

The curtains beside Zach's bed billowed in the cool spring breeze. The smell of fresh earth permeated his room. He remembered the feeling of that moist sod against his body when, as a kid, he lay in wait for groundhogs to crawl out of their dens. Spring was a time of renewal, he thought, maybe it was time for him to shed the past. Marta would have liked that. But how?

He put on his nightclothes and lay down. It occurred to him that all the years he had spent internalizing his post-Gettysburg experience, however horrible it may have been, might not have been the best way for him to cope with his memories. Maybe, just maybe, if he told his story, he could be done with it.

———

"Hello, Mr. Harkin? Are you here?" A voice yelled from outside.

"Keep your pants on. I'll be right down," Zach shouted, scrambling into his work overalls. He glanced at the clock: 10:00 am. He had never slept that late before.

He remembered what he had decided in the middle of the night. He would tell the whole story. He would tell everybody who would listen what had happened during those two years.

He opened the front door. "Mornin.' Martin isn't it?" Zach said. "Come on in. Guess I overslept."

Zach threw a few pieces of wood into the stove. "We'll have some hot coffee in a few minutes. Pull up a chair." The coals in the stove were still hot from the night before. Zach blew on them. The fire came alive and he went into the kitchen, poured coffee grounds in the bottom of the coffee pot, and added some water. The brew would be strong, but he had always preferred it to some of the modern percolators, which made the coffee bitter. Returning to the shop, he put the pot on the stove and sat down facing Chris.

"Suppose you're still looking for something for that paper of yours," he said.

"Only if you have the time," Martin said. He sat up straight in his chair and pushed back slightly, balancing on the chair's back legs, watching Zach. The stove let off a big pop and the fire made a whistling noise as it sucked in air through the vent.

"That is one luxury I have plenty of," Zach said. "Time. I suppose you want to know where I went after I disappeared back in sixty-four, and why."

"A lot of people do really want to know, especially those who care about you," the reporter said.

"I suppose you're right. I didn't get much sleep last night, thinking about it. This might be painful for me, but I think it's time for me to square things up with the world.

When I rode off into the night, gosh it was almost forty-seven years ago, wasn't it? I wanted to find the family of a Confederate sharpshooter I had killed and to tell them how sorry I was, but I never thought it would take so long to find them, and I had no idea how dangerous the journey was going to be."

3

Appalachian Foothills, Late Fall, 1863

A REDDISH-ORANGE SUN ROSE above the heavily-treed mountains to Zach's right as he rode away from Knoxville. His ears ached from the morning cold.

His horse was a big chestnut gelding with hooves the size of dinner plates. Zach thought it looked like an old warhorse, and it suited his needs perfectly. Zach had bought the horse from a Knoxville livery, and the choices had been few, as both sides of the war had either purchased or confiscated almost all the horses in the area.

He had packed his saddlebags with dried beef, coffee, hardtack, and a few cans of beans. Across the back of his saddle, he tied a blanket, hatchet, and poncho, all wrapped up in a waxed ground cloth. He was prepared to travel a long time.

Zach had left home in the middle of the night so he wouldn't have to explain himself to his parents. They would have tried to talk him out of whatever he intended to do. Of course, at the time, he didn't have a plan, but he was haunted by remorse, and the only thing he could think of was to try to find a way to make amends to the family of the sharpshooter. He had no idea what he would do if and when he found the lady in the picture, but he felt better just trying to do something about it.

Zach planned to ride through the night and next day to get over the Cumberland Gap before nightfall came again. Because of his aversion to any kind of firearm, he was unarmed. His discharge papers, signed by Colonel Berdan, lay folded at the bottom of one of his saddlebags.

Also, packed in his saddlebag was the dead man's forage cap. He thought it might help prove to the family that he wasn't an imposter trying to take advantage of a widow. Also, the inscription inside the cap, "McGowan's Brigade" was the only clue he had to the man's identity.

By late afternoon, Zach had traversed the gap, and the mountains receded into foothills. He had gotten used to the clump-clump of his big horse's hooves as it picked its way along the narrow passage. The sky had been clear all day, but as the sun set, thick ominous clouds portended the approach of a storm.

Zach made camp near a small creek under a big elm tree. He tethered his horse on a long rope and gathered firewood. As he prepared a place to sleep, he remembered camping with his father and the good times they had. So much had changed.

Zach rested his saddle up against the tree and lay down on his waxed ground cloth with his head on the saddle and his feet near the fire. The saddle smelled of leather, human sweat, and the distinctive musty pong of horse. He wondered what his parents thought when they found out he had left and regretted the worry they must be feeling. He cursed to himself. He could have at least left a note. He chewed on some hardtack and washed it down with water from his canteen. His eyelids became heavy, and he slept.

A loud crack of thunder and the simultaneous urgent whinny of his horse awoke him from a deep sleep. A sudden gust of wind blew hot embers from his campfire into some surrounding brush, which instantly caught fire. Zach ran over and secured his horse farther away, upwind, and when he returned, the fire was spreading fast through the brush. He beat the flames with his blanket, but they were over six feet high by then and his efforts had little effect. Thick smoke with the smell of burning underbrush burned Zach's nose and throat and stung his eyes, forcing him to stand away. Bolts of lightning pierced the sky, accompanied by earsplitting thunder. The fire raged toward the creek, with the wind acting like a bellows, sending plumes of smoke across the countryside.

Then the rain came. First, large drops, almost horizontal on the wind, stung his face. As the drops hit the fire, they made a hissing sound, then popped like bacon frying in a skillet. The rain increased, stifling the flames and sending up even more smoke. Lightning lit the sky and Zach could see the clouds of smoke moving up the mountainside.

The wind died down, and the rain became a deluge, dousing the fire and turning the ground to mud.

Zach huddled under the elm with his ground cloth over his head. The temperature dropped and he shivered. The raindrops turned to a fine mist then stopped completely as the storm moved on and the air became still. He wrapped himself with his blanket, then with his ground cloth, and lay down. The only thing Zach could hear were heavy drops of water falling off the trees onto soaked leaves. The smell of wet earth and ashes hung in the air. Zach slept.

The early morning light wove its way through the trees as Zach awoke, cold, damp, and hungry. He rolled out of his blanket and stood up. His body ached from the hard ground and dampness. He decided he needed to start a fire to dry everything out before he traveled on. With his hatchet, he removed the wet bark from several dead tree limbs he had gathered, exposing the dry centers. He cut the limbs into small pieces and propped them like a tepee near where his previous fire had been. Then he carefully cut shavings and formed a thick ball. Striking two pieces of flint together, he made sparks, and after many tries, one of the sparks ignited the shavings. Holding the shavings in his hand, he gently blew on the tiny flame and placed it under the tepee of firewood. He continued to blow, and the flame grew and ignited the larger limbs. Smoke rose as the little fire gained strength. Zach squatted beside the fire with his hands spread out to warm them. He always felt a sense of satisfaction when he made a fire, and this one had been tougher than usual.

The sound of Zach's horse chewing on grass suddenly stopped. It's head turned to the south with its ears pointing alertly at something it heard in the distance. Then Zach heard it, also—the sound of approaching horses and rattling sabers.

He grabbed his saddle and ran toward his horse, but it was too late to escape. Six men rode into his camp and surrounded him. Their horses pranced and stomped, gnashing their bits as the riders pulled on the reins. They were lathered, breathing hard, their breath forming puffs of vapor, which rose in the thick morning air. The riders' uniforms were gray.

The lead horseman, a sergeant, judging by the three stripes on his shoulder, said with a deep drawl, "A young feller like you roaming these here parts can only be a Yankee sympathizer or a goddamn deserter." He leaned forward with both hands on his saddle horn and said with a sneer, "Which are you, mister?" The man's red hair looked like a bird's nest with a forage cap on top. His red beard was stained and unkempt. His teeth were stained almost green, and the side of his cheek bulged with tobacco.

The rider next to the one with stripes said, "Makes no difference if he's a deserter or a sympathizer. We'll hang him either way. Right, Sarge?" He reached back and untied a rope from his saddle and made a loop, grinning. He was hatless, his stringy dark hair hung down to his shoulders. He had a scar on his right cheek that extended past a hole where his right ear once was.

Zach silently cursed himself for not having prepared an answer to such a question. He decided to tell the truth. "I was on the Union side for a while, but I was discharged," he said.

"Likely story. Do you expect us to believe that?" Another said.

"Show us your discharge papers," the sergeant said. "Bet you don't have 'em, do ya?"

Zach thought about it briefly, then said, "They're in my saddlebag." He leaned over to open the bag, and as he did, a third soldier pushed him hard, knocking him to the ground.

"We'll do the looking, you deserting son-of-a-bitch," the man with one ear said, dismounting. He grabbed the bags and turned them upside down. Everything came tumbling out: beans, hardtack, coffee. Seeing no discharge papers, the man said, "Just as we thought. No damn papers in here. Time to string him up. Let's do it."

"Hold on a minute, Harris," the sergeant said, dismounting. He looked through the saddlebags, pulled out some papers that had been wedged in the bottom, and opened them up. He studied them, his finger pointing to each word. He went over the text again, his forehead wrinkled. Finally, he said to the others, "Well it's a discharge sure enough. It's signed by Colonel Hiram Berdan of the U.S. Sharpshooters."

When the others heard "sharpshooters," they all stiffened as if they had seen a rattlesnake hiding in rocks. For a moment, they were quiet, until finally the sergeant said, "You're one of those bastards?"

"Let's hang the son-of a-bitch. This tree right here should do. C'mon, Sarge. This guy isn't even worth taking prisoner," Harris said, in an anxious tone. "Let's do it now and get going. We got ground to cover."

Zach realized things were getting out of hand. "You're making a mistake," Zach said. "I no longer want to fight. I'm just riding…" He lay there, looking up at his assailants.

"Shut up you lowdown scoundrel," Harris said. "Here, try this on." He slipped the loop over Zach's head. He pulled it taut and threw the other end over a low limb of the elm. "This should do it. Somebody get his horse."

The sergeant stroked his short beard, deep in thought. "Wait a minute, boys. This man has only recently been discharged. He might have some information we can use. We don't get many sharpshooter prisoners. Maybe we should take him in and see what the captain wants to do."

The others looked disappointed. As though somebody had just denied them a shot of whiskey.

"Yep, that's what we're gonna do. We'll take him in, and if the captain has no use for him, we'll string him up then—hang him high. We can wait a couple hours. We need to be sure. He looked at Zach, "Get your sorry ass up. And by the way, you ain't got but a few hours left to live." He spat a stream of dark brown fluid, which landed near Zach's feet.

4

Knoxville, Tennessee, 1908

"LOOKS LIKE A serious conversation," a man said, coming in the front door.

"Mornin', Judge. Come on in. Its ready," Zach said, and disappeared into the next room.

The judge was a short, rotund man. He went to the stove and poured himself a cup of coffee, eyeing Chris. "You a stranger in these parts?" he asked.

"Yes, I'm here from *The New York World*. Zach and I have been talking about the war."

Glancing at the doorway, the judge said, "Well, that doesn't happen very often."

Zach returned, holding a rifle. "Here it is, Judge. Just what you ordered. Hope you like it."

The judge took the gun with an admiring gleam in his eye. "I'd better like it. You're charging me enough for it." He winked and gave a wry smile. The rifle was a bolt action Springfield 30.06 with a custom, hand-checked stock. The modified clip held eight cartridges instead of the usual five. He slowly ran his fingers over the stock, then carefully sheathed the gun in his holster. He thanked Zach and left, still with a smile on his face.

Chris returned to the hotel.

"Lunch?" he asked Jerome, who was behind the counter.

"You buyin'?"

The dining room was crowded with women. Jerome said it was the monthly meeting of the Daughters of the American Revolution. They wore fine dresses and many wore flowered hats with broad brims. Their conversations were lively. Jerome and Chris had to speak up so they could hear each other.

Before Chris had left New York, he'd read as much as was available about Zach's military career. He learned that Zach had been mustered out just before the Battle of Gettysburg because he was unable to fire at the enemy. He was discharged and sent home. Then he disappeared and nobody knew what happened.

Chris asked Jerome about Zach's social life after he was discharged.

"Stayed home, mostly," Jerome said. "I guess he just kept to his room. His folks couldn't figure it out. Before the war, he was always doing something: hunting, working, shooting. He was always out and about. Such a big change in his behavior in such a short period of time really worried them, especially his mom."

He didn't go out at all?" Chris asked.

"Once. An old school friend of his came over one day and asked Zach if he wanted to go hunting. Zach didn't want to, but his mother encouraged him, and he reluctantly went along, without a gun. I guess his friend said something to the effect that the only good Rebel was a dead Rebel, and Zach hit him in the face so hard it knocked him out. Zach left him lying on the ground and went back to his room. Like I said, Zach was a big boy and everybody presumed he could handle himself, but this was strange. He had never even been in a light scuffle before that I know of. Several days later, he left."

"How do you know all of this?"

"Well, the other guy didn't say a word to anybody right away. Guess he was embarrassed. But after Zach left, he told friends what had happened, and it all became general knowledge soon thereafter."

Chris went back to his room to write the first installment of Zach's story.

5

Appalachian Mountains, 1864

O N FOOT, WITH his hands tied behind him and the noose around his neck, Zach was forced to walk behind the mounted Rebels as they headed to the southeast. "Either keep up with us or we'll drag you by the neck," Harris had said, tying the other end of the rope around his saddle horn.

The horses were kept at a fast walk, and Zach had to almost trot to keep up. The rough hemp rope chafed his neck. He cursed himself for not having been more cautious. When the fire had spread the night before, the smoke must have alerted the soldiers to his presence. He had been careless, and he vowed never to let that happen again—if he ever got the chance.

The morning wore on as they clambered over a little-used trail. Zach's legs tired quickly. He could not use his hands and arms to keep his balance. He had to watch every step.

Zach asked for a rest, his voice raspy, and the sergeant decided to stop. He told Harris to guard Zach while the rest of the party scouted ahead to see if they could find others who were patrolling the area.

As the scouting party rode off, Harris approached Zach with a sneer on his face. "Won't be long now," he said, "till you're hanging from a tree. Just swinging back and forth. Then, you won't be able to breathe, your neck will be broken, and you will know how it feels to die." He came close to Zach's face, leering. His breath was ripe and disgusting. His uniform reeked of sweat, and food streaked down the front. Tobacco juice oozed down his chin, absorbed by his straggly beard.

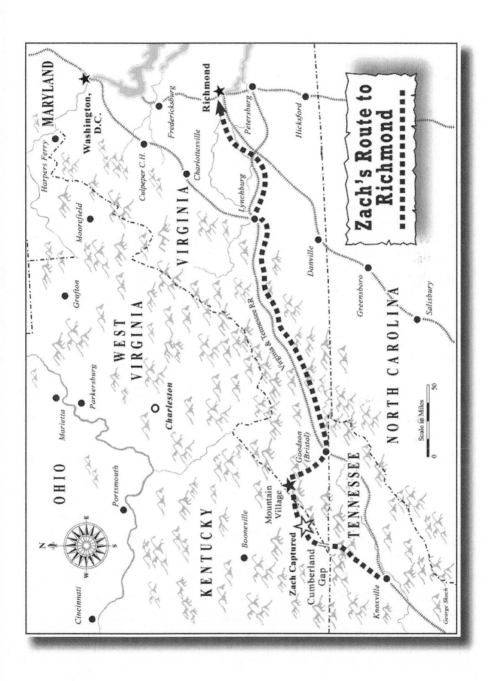

"The only good Yankee's a dead one," he said, and he spat, hitting Zach between his eyes.

Zach backed away. Unable to wipe the spittle off his face, he felt rage rising in his chest.

Almost instinctively, he put his head down and charged the man with all the energy he had, hitting him in the soft spot just below his sternum. The man went down hard and gasped for breath. Zach kicked him in the same spot, knocking him unconscious. He stood over the man, wanting to kill him, but first he had to free his hands.

He ran his foot over Harris' pockets, hoping to find a knife. Finding none, he looked around for a sharp rock that he might use to saw the ropes loose. There were none. He knew the others in the group would be back soon and he considered just running into the woods and hiding. Then it came to him. The man's saber. He inserted the toe of his shoe in the unconscious man's saber handle and eased it out of its sheath. He lay down next to it, clasped his tied hands on the hilt, and stood up. Then he managed to stick the point of the saber into the ground and sat down with his back to the blade, sawing at the ropes. Finally, his hands were free.

The soldier started to moan, and Zach kicked him one more time.

He felt it before he heard it—searing pain flared in his side like a red-hot ember. The rifle crack sounded immediately after, along with the clack of shod hooves approaching fast. The men had returned.

The captain dismounted. Looking first at the unconscious soldier lying on the ground, then to the saber sticking in the dirt, and finally at Zach, he said, "Looks like Harris got outsmarted again. Don't know if he'll ever learn." He motioned for all to dismount, then pointed at the sergeant and said, "Check Harris out. I want to take a look at this sharpshooter."

He put his boot against Zach's head, pushing it up so he could see his face. He stared in disbelief. "Well, I'll be. I'll, goddamned to hell, be." He looked up at the others. "We got ourselves somebody here, boys. I can't believe it. Jesus H. Christ. We went to school together."

"A deserter, huh?" The sergeant said.

"No, this here man is none other than Zachary Harkin from Knoxville," the captain said.

"Never heard of him, Captain"

"You are even dumber than you look. This is the sharpshooter who shot Albert Sidney Johnston. He's a legend in these parts." The captain leaned over to check Zach's wound. "He's been shot in the side here. He's lost some blood but it doesn't look like much more than a surface wound." He stood and scratched his head. "Guess we'll take him back to headquarters for some questioning. How's Harris?"

"Broken ribs, maybe. He'll live," the sergeant said.

"Put Harris and him on horses. Let's get out of here," the captain said.

They rode through the mountains the rest of the day. Some of the trails were narrow and forced them to proceed in single file. Zach's wound stopped bleeding. The blood on his shirt had dried, sticking to the open wound like a scab. The sky was clear and the air cool from the storm the night before. The sun felt warm. Zach had plenty of time to ponder his situation. He hoped to escape, but as they got closer to the Rebel headquarters, he knew his chances were diminishing.

They descended into a valley and entered a tiny village constructed in a clearing with a handful of shabby homes. The windows had no glass, and seemed to be covered in animal skins. The clapboard walls looked like they had never seen a coat of paint, and some boards were entirely missing, leaving gaping holes, some of which were stuffed with newspaper. Weeds grew shoulder high between the buildings. A narrow path led into the trees, where an outhouse could be seen, the door of which hung at an angle, supported by only one hinge.

The captain held up his hand, stopping the group, and dismounted. Through an open door of one of the houses, Zach could see a dirt floor, two chairs, and a table. The table was piled with dirty dishes and food scraps covered with flies.

Three young girls came out of another of the hovels to see the newcomers. They seemed to be sisters. All three wore threadbare cotton dresses. Zach guessed that the tallest one was around sixteen and the other two, a bit younger. Their hair was straight and unkempt, though the oldest girl had two pigtails holding hers out of her face.

They were wide-eyed and curious. The older girl noticed that Zach's arms were tied. She looked at the captain, "S'cuse me Mister Officer, but ain't that a Yankee?" She pointed at Zach. "A real live Yankee?"

The captain chuckled, and said, "Sure 'nuff, girl. Ain't you seen one before?"

"Ne'er one as handsome as this one," she said. She eyed Zach with a lusty boldness that unnerved him.

The other girls pointed and giggled, but seemed more shy.

"And the size of those hands," she continued. "My, oh my."

The captain seemed to be enjoying himself. "Want a better look?" He motioned to one of the other soldiers. "Get this man down, so these fine young ladies can get a good look at 'im."

Zach's face burned crimson as the girls walked around him, snickering and pointing, as if he was some kind of freak. The oldest girl pointed at Zach's feet, "Just look at the size of those shoes," she said. "Takes a big man to fill those shoes. I mean, a really big man." The others giggled even more. "Goodness, a man with such big hands and big arms? My, oh my." She stood in front of Zach, her eyes roving from his head to his feet, then back up to his mid-section. "Oh my, I just wonder…" she said. The other two could barely contain their mirth.

Zach's embarrassment turned to anger.

"Can he talk?" the older one asked.

The sergeant dismounted. "Sure he can talk," he said. Then, looking directly at Zach, his voice became derisive, "Why don't you tell these young ladies what you were doin' in these parts, anyway."

Zach stiffened. He felt like a slab of bacon hanging in a butcher shop.

"Maybe he should sing," the first girl said, holding her hand over her mouth to cover her crooked teeth.

"Yes! Yes, let's hear him sing!" another girl said.

All eyes were on Zach.

The sergeant put his face in front of Zach's. He had to look up because Zach was much taller. "Listen, you stinkin' bastard. You either sing or we'll string you up right here in front of these fine ladies. Now sing."

"Maybe Yankees can't sing," the older girl said. "Maybe they just grunt."

Zach could see the hatred in the sergeant's eyes, but he wasn't going to sing. He studied the man's face, noticed the bloodshot eyes, the bulging veins in his temples, the slight quivering of his eyelids. Zach could see the fear in his eyes.

Zach's anger had its own set of rules. Forgetting the girls and the other soldiers, he watched the sergeant.

"You gonna make him sing, ain't ya, Sarge?" one of the soldiers said.

The sergeant grinned and faced Zach. With all the strength he could muster, Zach snapped his knee up, catching the sergeant squarely in the groin. The sergeant was not a small man, but Zach's kick lifted him into the air. The sergeant's look changed from one of contempt to one of pain, and he crumpled to the ground, clutching his crotch. The girls screamed and ran. The soldiers, slow to react, closed in on Zach, one hitting him hard on the head with the butt of his rifle, knocking him unconscious.

––––––––

Zach had been awake for hours when the morning sun started to spill over the eastern hills onto the town of Goodson, Virginia like light through a slowly opened door. The fall leaves shone blood red, crimson, and gold. Zach's hands and feet were bound and his torso draped over a saddle. Each step of the horse amplified the ache in his head from the blow he'd received the night before. Several times, he had fainted, only to be awakened again by the jarring motion of the horse. His body was numb. He wished he could faint again. He tried to clear his head, to think. He could feel wetness on his side, and reasoned that rubbing against the saddle had opened the gunshot wound.

When he looked back, he could see Harris on horseback, wincing, his broken ribs wrapped in a cloth. Harris stared at Zach with hatred and Zach was at least thankful he was not currently capable of retaliation. Zach knew he would have killed Harris had he not been shot. He didn't know what had come over him, but he didn't like it.

The captain ordered them to stop, and one of the men untied Zach's legs. They pulled him off the horse, and he stood. He fought to stay conscious. He was in the center of Goodson. A sign on the building in front of him read, "The Exchange Hotel," which was being used as a Confederate hospital.

The captain approached a group of officers gathered across the street. Several minutes later, he returned and told the sergeant to take Zach to the train station. He was going to Belle Isle in Richmond. "And may he rot in hell," he said.

6

Richmond, Virginia, 1864

THE SIGN OVER the entrance read: "THOMAS LIBBY & SON— SHIP CHANDLERS AND GROCERS."

This was the notorious Libby Prison.

Zach and sixteen other prisoners entered the prison office, where several clerks recorded names, ranks, and regiments into their logbooks. The prisoners could hear each other being questioned, and when Zach said he had been with the U.S. Sharpshooters, many took notice. The recording clerk asked him how to spell "sharpshooter."

They had seemingly never processed one before.

The prisoners were then lined up to be searched for weapons, items that could be used as weapons, and valuables.

The other sixteen prisoners were from the Third Union Corps, captured at the Battle of Mine Run. Serving under Brigadier General William H. Morris, they had been largely untested going into the battle. These prisoners were all from New York, and while the Third Corps was mostly responsible for the Union loss, they all appeared cocky, staying apart from the others. They ignored Zach and talked among themselves in a broken English that Zach had trouble understanding. The man doing the searching was referred to as Majah Turnah. He was short, fat, wore a thin goatee, and his tallow-colored skin was covered with sweat. His beady eyes shifted from one thing to another, as if he was worried he would miss something. As each prisoner stood in front of him, he asked for valuables, and peered into their eyes, as if to determine if he was being lied to. Almost all the New Yorkers denied having anything, but he thoroughly searched each of them. He searched under armpits, between legs, and even ran his fingers through their hair. He was not gentle and did not care where he put his hands. He searched everywhere. Whatever he found that might be of value, he slid into his pocket.

Zach was last in line and when the major finally got to him, Zach told him he had nothing valuable. Turner looked up at him and hesitated. Zach held his gaze, and after several moments, Turner nodded his head, motioning him to move on. As he did, Turner's hand brushed Zach's rear pocket. "Wait a minute. Stop right here. What this?" He reached into Zach's pocket and pulled out the dead man's logbook. He seemed disappointed.

"That's personal," Zach said.

"Personal? Personal?" Turner stood. "Look, mister, when you come through that door right there, you become mine. You are all mine. You don't have any 'personal.' You belong to me and don't you ever forget it." The major's fat fingers pointed menacingly at Zach. Sweat dripped off the man's fat face, soaking his collar.

The boys from New York snickered.

Turner leafed through the little logbook. "Is this yours?" he asked, reading a couple of entries. Then he came to the photo of the woman. "Is this your wife? Your sweetheart?" He read on, his voice becoming louder. "Are you a deserter, a Confederate? Speak up, soldier. What the hell is this all about?"

The room went quiet. Even the clerks stopped and stared.

Zach wasn't sure where the questioning was going, so he decided to tell the truth. "I was discharged from duty. That logbook belongs to a dead soldier I saw on the battlefield. I just wanted to return it to his family. That's all."

The major ran his finger across his forehead and shook the sweat off on the side. His face was turning red as the inside of a watermelon. "Let me get this straight. You say you were discharged, but now you want to go to a dead man's house? To do what? Tell the family the man is dead? And you are willing to risk being captured to do it? Are you crazy?"

The major looked at the picture of the woman again. A faint, knowing smile, almost a sneer, came over his face. He said, in a low voice, as if slowly comprehending, "You dirty son of a bitch. You lowlife bastard. You want to plug his wife! The poor mourning widow! Now, I have heard it all. You god-damned Yankees are all the same. You are one sorry ass."

Zach felt his face flush and his chest pound. His anger turned to rage. The man in front of him didn't, couldn't, wouldn't understand. Just as he was about to grab the man by the shirt and throw him against the wall, the major said, "Sergeant! The smell in here reminds me of a shit house. Get these worthless goddamned Yankees out of here. I've got better things to do."

The sergeant, anxious to defuse the situation, ushered the men back out into the street. He instructed another soldier to take the New Yorkers to a building next door. Then he told Zach he was being assigned to the second floor of the Pemberton Building on the corner of 15th and Carey Streets.

The sergeant was an older man. Too old for field duty. As they walked, he said softly, "Glad to get you out of there before things got out of hand. I sensed the major got under your skin. He can do that. He gets pretty mean at times. Doesn't have a friend in the world. All he wants is money, and he'll do whatever it takes to get it, if you know what I mean."

Zach had cooled down, and he welcomed the sergeant's friendly tone. On a whim, he said, "Sergeant, have you ever heard of McGowan's Brigade?"

The sergeant pushed the bill of his cap up as if to help himself think, "South Carolina, I believe. Yep, South Carolina. Hmm, Sam McGowan. That who you're looking for?"

"Not sure, but thanks. I'm looking for the family of a man who was killed near Chancellorsville."

They approached a group of guards standing in front of a three-story brick building. The sergeant told one of them to take Zach up to the second floor. Just before the sergeant walked away, he whispered to Zach, "I'll check around and see what I can find out."

———

Zach tried to adjust to the daily routine of prison life. The heavy smell of tobacco permeated the whole building and helped mask the smell of unbathed men. His floor housed over three hundred Union prisoners, none of whom were officers. Almost all on his floor were from the Army of the Potomac, and they tended to be divided into two groups: proponents and opponents of their general, George McClellan. The opponents thought McClellan was a procrastinator and grandstander, afraid to make a decisive move, always waiting, preparing, and complaining that he didn't have enough men and resources. In their eyes, the war would have been over long ago and they would be back with their families if only they had a real leader. The proponents saw McClellan as a godlike general who could do no wrong. A soldier's soldier. A master strategist.

Other differences defined groups of men, such as cavalry versus foot soldiers. The cavalrymen considered themselves superior, while the infantrymen thought they did all the hard fighting while the cavalry had light duty, riding around on horses all day. Some of the men were veterans. They were referred to as "first call." They had been in service from the beginning of the war. Others had joined up later and were frequently dubbed "three hundred dollar soldiers" because they had been paid by the U.S. government to enlist.

Zach didn't fall into any of these groups. He preferred to be alone anyway, and rarely entered into conversations with the others. When he first arrived on the second floor, he was greeted by the other prisoners, as all newcomers were, with questions about the war. He shared with them what he knew. However, most of his knowledge was dated, and they quickly left him alone. They were indifferent to his sharpshooter service, and he did not tell them about any of his experiences at Shiloh and Chancellorsville.

Each morning, the guards held rollcall. All the prisoners would fall into four ranks and a diminutive Rebel soldier with a notebook, accompanied by two guards, took careful count of each one. After that, they would wait three hours for mess, at noon, which would be their only meal of the day. Just before mess, a guard would yell for the sergeant of the floor to assemble fourteen prisoners to go outside to the cookhouse to get the rations for the entire floor. Everybody wanted to be one of the fourteen, if for no other reason than to briefly be outside. They would return, and the food would be distributed, after which the men had nothing to do for the rest of the day.

The second floor had seven windows, all facing south, offering a good view of the James River and the Kanawha Canal. To the distant south, Fort Darling was visible atop Drewry's Bluff. The fort, with its guns positioned one hundred feet above the river, protected Richmond from naval attacks. Immediately in front of the windows and across the river was a flat, sandy plain that was used as the proving ground for the cannons cast at the Tredegar Iron Works, not far away. During the day, viewing space was crowded with men.

Zach remembered swimming across the Rappahanock in the middle of the night, the cold water, and the waiting for the man who had shot his friend. The spider lines centered on the man's head, the controlled breathing, squeezing the trigger, then the sight of the man's splintered jaw. Blood and bone fragments plastered against the tree. The logbook with the woman's photograph.

He thought of the widow, now left alone. Possibly a young child who now had no father because of him and his goddamned rifle.

The image of the dead sharpshooter still appeared almost every night. When he was home, the image appeared on the edge of his bed. In prison, the apparition would sit on the bare floor beside him. In his melancholy, Zach sat with his head against the wall for hours. At first, other prisoners tried to talk to him, but Zach resisted, continuing to stare into nothing.

7

Knoxville, Tennessee, 1906

ZACH BURIED HIS face in his hands.

"Must have been pure hell," Chris said.

"After all these years, the pain hasn't diminished. I still see Jack at the foot of my bed most nights."

"Jack?"

"Yep, his name was Jack Kavandish. Thanks to me, his son never knew his father's embrace. I destroyed that for him."

"But I heard he shot your friend, Myron," Chris said.

"Myron was younger, single, no family was ruined. I'm sure life got back to normal in quick order for Myron's parents. What I did was much worse than what he did. It doesn't compare."

"You're being too hard on yourself," Chris said. "War is hell, as Sherman once said. People do things they wouldn't normally do in peacetime. Just imagine how many soldiers did what you did. There cannot be any blame." Chris felt uncomfortable trying to soothe Zach's feelings. He was a reporter. He was here to learn the story, not try to change it, but Zach's deep sorrow was so real, and he had harbored those feelings for so many years. Chris felt like he had to say something.

"Tell me a more about Confederate prisons," Chris said, starting his third notebook.

Zach tried to explain the circumstances prevailing in the Confederacy at that time. In the years since his captivity, he had wanted to understand why the cruelties occurred, in an effort to forgive. He told Chris that in November of 1863, the Confederate Secretary of War, James Seddon, instructed Captain William Winder to find a suitable location for a large new prison. A prison safely buried in the South, so Union forces could not reach it easily. After several attempts, Winder found a suitable place near the village of Andersonville, Georgia. Originally named Camp Sumter, after the county in which it was located, it was popularly called Andersonville. The prison was easily accessible by the Central Georgia Rail Line, through Macon from points north. It was located on sixteen acres with a stream running through called Sweetwater Creek, which was later renamed Stockade Branch. The prison was built to hold ten thousand prisoners.

He explained that by early 1864, when he was in Libby Prison, Richmond held over fifteen thousand prisoners at Belle Isle, Castle Thunder, Castle Lightning, Libby, and others. Officials in Richmond perceived a threat to the civilian population should a mass escape occur, possibly resulting in the rape of their women and the freeing of their slaves. One out of every five people living in Richmond was a prisoner. Food had already become scarce, and railroad service was on the decline due to loss of rail, locomotives, and railcars. The prisoners were a drain on the city's dwindling resources.

When Chris returned to his room later that day, a telegram had been slipped under his door. His editor, Robert Hunt Lyman, told him his first article had been popular and *The World's* readers were anxious to read more about Zach Harkin. Usually, when on assignment, Chris's communications with the paper were through one of the editorial staff. This telegram, direct from Lyman, was telling.

Chris sat down at the little table and wrote the second installment. When it was completed, he lay his six-foot frame down on the bed, put his hands behind his head, and thought about what he knew of Zach's story so far.

Chris was from Bartow County, in northeastern Georgia, just on the other side of the Appalachians from where Zach lived. Chris's father's home and plantation were burned by Union forces in 1864 as the Federal Armies of Tennessee and Cumberland laid waste to the area. Chris' father always blamed Sherman for the willful and utter devastation, the economic effects of which were still apparent. His slaves freed, and his crops destroyed, his father died a broken man, bitter to the end.

The next morning, Chris found Zach anxious to continue his story.

8

Richmond, Virginia, 1864

A GUARD ZACH HAD not seen before came to the top of the steps on the third floor and announced in a loud voice, "All you damn Yankees on the second floor have one hour to get ready. You are being transferred!"

A cheer rose among the men and built to a boisterous crescendo. To everyone on the floor "transfer" meant exchange. The magical word they all hoped to hear. The prisoners yelled, cheered, and danced. Several got down on their knees, their eyes cast upwards, thanking the Lord for finally answering their prayers. One man slapped the man next to him on the back so hard, he fell to the floor, laughing.

Zach gathered his few belongings, carefully stowing the logbook in his back pocket. He had noticed that when they had cleared out the building, readying it to become a prison, they'd left small sheets of metal nestled in the rafters. On a whim, he grabbed a dozen or so and tucked them under the bib of his overalls.

The hour-long wait turned into five, but prisoners were finally asked to line up two-by-two. They marched down the stairs and into the sun and fresh air. Once all three hundred were outside, they were required to wait another hour before they were marched to the train station. Among the guards was the same man who had escorted Zach to his building on the first day. He approached Zach and simply said, "Abbeville, South Carolina." Before Zach could respond, he disappeared.

By late afternoon, the prisoners were all loaded on the train. They were squeezed so tightly into the car that no one could move. The car, recently used to transport stock animals, had a wooden floor and wooden slat sides. The old animal excrement on the unwashed floorboards burned Zach's nose as the guards kept adding more and more prisoners. Zach could not walk or bend his knees. Simply turning around was nearly impossible. The man next to him was panting, his arms flailing, striking the men around him. Even though the air was cool, the man's upturned face was slick with sweat. He mumbled, "I gotta get outta here." Then again, slightly louder, his breathing becoming more erratic. "I gotta get outta of here!"

The train started to move with a jolt and the occupants of the car jerked toward the back. Now pressed together even more tightly.

"I gotta get outta here!" the man screamed, his eyes wide and bulging. He managed to raise his arms into the air and the space vacated by his arms was filled immediately by the men around him, like air rushing into a vacuum. Zach was taller than most of the others. He managed to turn and face the man, whose back was to him. He put his arms around him and whispered in his ear, "It's going to be okay. Calm down. We're all in this together."

The man turned his contorted face toward Zach. "I can't stand it. I gotta get out of here!"

Zach started to lift him up. "Help me out a little here," he said to the others as he struggled to hoist the man higher. The others in the car tried to give him room, and with slightly more space, Zach was able to lift the man higher, so his waist was above the shoulders of the rest of them. Freeing the man's arms seemed to calm him.

"Any better?" Zach asked.

"I guess so," the man said, his voice still trembling.

After several minutes, Zach said, "I'm going to lower you down. Just stay calm, okay, now?"

The man nodded, his breathing almost normal.

Some of the other prisoners were murmuring that the train was still heading south. They had hoped the exchange would take place on the outskirts of Richmond, but the train had already passed there. Somebody said they were headed to Petersburg and surely the exchange would take place there and spirits were raised again.

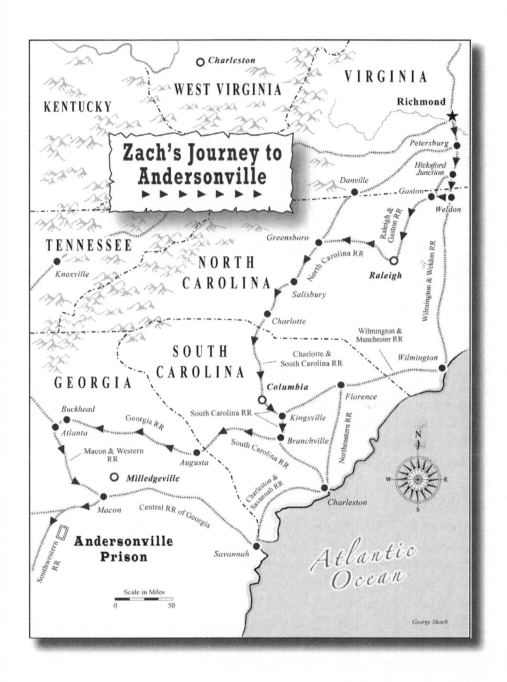

Several hours later, the train stopped in Petersburg, the brakes squealing, metal on metal, and the men were thrust forward as one. They waited for the doors to open, but after almost an hour, the train slowly chugged away.

Zach estimated they had been in the crowded car for well over eight hours with no water, food, or relief of any kind. The men had grown quiet, as if mesmerized by the rhythm of the wheels and the gentle swaying of the cars.

The acrid smell of fresh urine and human excrement spread through the car. Zach could feel wetness through his clothing from the man next to him. He could feel the legs of the men around him yield to weariness and their bodies would wedge themselves against his like the stones of an arched doorway, unable to fall.

They stopped in Columbia to change trains. Railroads in the South lacked the uniformity of northern railroads. Some had tracks five feet across while others were wider or narrower. The five-foot gauge, sometimes called the "broad gauge" was used because a cotton bale was five feet wide and fit perfectly. Zach's train could not run on more than one gauge, so they had to be off-loaded, then reloaded at each gauge change.

As the train emptied, the prisoners were given crackers and water and then loaded into another set of cars on a different track. Each car held approximately one hundred-thirty prisoners, and as they boarded, a guard asked the prisoner closest to the door for a headcount. When the guard was satisfied the car was at maximum capacity, he would move to the next. When it was Zach's turn to board, he climbed in with the man who had panicked next to him, and quickly counted fifty men. He had an idea.

"Okay, you men! Crowd around the door as tight as you can," he instructed.

When the guard tried to put more in the car, Zach yelled, "We have too many. We are already jammed too tight."

The guard asked how many, and Zach took a moment, then replied that they had over a hundred and thirty men. The guard looked up, saw the crowd around the door, and moved on. The men were all smiles as the train departed, heading southwest. They had plenty of room to lie down, and most slept in the front of the car. Later that day, the train stopped, and Zach could see that rations were being handed out to each car. Zach again instructed the men to crowd around the door. When it was opened, the guards handed out rations for one hundred-thirty, and when the door was closed again, the happy prisoners enjoyed double rations. All eyed Zach with appreciation.

A relaxed mood settled over the boxcar. The men sat, leaning against the sides of the car, facing each other.

One asked Zach, "What unit were you with?"

"Not with any unit," Zach said.

"You discharged?"

"You might say that."

"If you don't mind my asking, where were you when you were discharged?"

"Gettysburg."

"Well, don't that beat all? We were in Gettysburg, too. Third Michigan Volunteers. We were in the Peach Orchard. Never want to go back there again. We lost a lot of men. Goddamnedest battle I ever seen. We had them, though. We were solid. Could have ended the war right there if old Snapping Turtle Meade would have finished Lee off on the fourth day. We'd be home right now, nice and warm, enjoying good home cooked food. Yesiree."

Zach just stared at his feet.

Another man asked, "What unit were you with at Gettysburg?"

Zach said he didn't want to talk about it.

A steady, cold rain came down as the train hissed to a stop early the next morning. Zach could see a sign on the small depot station, Andersonville. One of the guards walked down the line of cars, unlocking the doors, and at each door he ordered the men out. The date was February 28, 1865. The journey from Richmond had taken seven days. The prisoners were cold, stiff, and hungry, but certain they had finally reached their destination. The mood matched the gloomy weather. They all sensed that what was coming could not be good.

They had only marched a short distance when they came to a giant fortress wall of vertical logs in the middle of which were two large, hinged doors that opened with a low, hollow groan. As the men entered the stockade, they could see that it was unfinished. Only three palisades had been constructed, and the fourth consisted of a battery of cannon aimed inward, threatening anyone who would dare try to escape. The doors through which they had entered were on top of a rise that sloped down to a small, swampy looking creek, then up again to the far wall. The walls enclosed an area of about fifteen acres. The guards only gave the prisoners a cursory inspection, believing they had already been inspected in their prior internments. Each man's name was recorded, along with his unit, and whether the man had a special trade. All the men were divided into groups of ninety, called messes, and were put in the charge of a sergeant whose duties included rollcall and the draw of rations.

Zach reported his unit as the United States Sharpshooters, and when asked if he had a special trade, he told them he was a gunsmith. While the guards were particularly foul of mouth, they seemed almost friendly, even kind at times. They were professional soldiers, mainly from the Fifty-fifth, Fifty-sixth, and Fifty-seventh Georgia, along with others from the Twenty-sixth Alabama.

The guards left the prisoners alone once they were inside the gates. No shelter, no supervision, no tents, no imposed organization. A few hundred prisoners were already there, and they had made ragtag tents and lean-tos from blankets, sticks, and whatever materials they had. The new arrivals were stunned by what they saw, but icy rain continued to fall, and they scrambled to construct shelters.

A few prisoners tried to make Zach's acquaintance, but he eschewed company and remained to himself. The others formed up teams of two, three or more to make shelters. He scanned the area on both sides of the main doors. Almost all the high, dry spots suitable for a makeshift tent had been taken. A young boy wearing a fez hat and striped, baggy trousers sat by himself amidst the makeshift tents. The boy had his arms wrapped around himself. He was soaking wet, shivering, and staring at the ground. Zach stooped down, put his hand on the boy's back, and said, "You look lonesome."

The boy looked up at him. He had a freckled face and pleading, dark brown eyes. He looked only briefly at Zach, then turned his attention back to the ground.

"I'm going to build a tent. Want me to make it big enough for two? You can help. We'll do it together."

The boy did not respond.

"Okay, you guard this spot. I'll go out and find some material for our tent. Don't let anybody take our spot, okay?"

Zach walked down to the creek, where some bushes grew. He saw three others scavenging there. One was the man who had panicked earlier in the boxcar. The man was chopping a small tree with a hatchet, and when he saw Zach, his eyes lit up.

"Where did you get the hatchet?" Zach asked.

"We were lucky, I guess. Several of us from the Third Michigan were allowed to keep them after we used them on special duty outside the gates several days ago. Guess the guard must have had a soft spot for us. Here, you need one? We have another."

Zach thanked him and quickly cut a series of saplings eight to ten feet long. Then he cut a bunch of shorter ones and trimmed them of their limbs and leaves. He returned the hatchet, then gathered everything up and walked back uphill.

Halfway there, his foot slipped, and he fell onto the red, slippery mud, and his load went flying as he tried to break his fall. When he stood, his clothes and hands were covered in red mud. He reflexively wiped his brow and the mud came off his hands onto his face.

Dropping the saplings on the ground near the boy, he said, "Here is the start of our new home." The boy looked up, saw his clothes, and a smile appeared on his face. He pointed at Zach and broke into laughter. Zach, realizing what he must look like, started to laugh, also. He sat next to the boy and both howled with laughter as the rain continued to fall.

Zach started construction. He took one of his longest saplings, stuck one end securely in the wet earth, and bent it around, forming a "U." He secured the other end the same way. "This is our front door," Zach said, watching the boy. Hoping for a response. The boy remained silent, but attentive.

Zach bent another sapling into a "U" about six feet away and formed the rear of the shelter. Then he filled in the space between them with a bent sapling every six inches or so.

"What's your name, son?" Zach asked. "You must have a name. Mine is Zach. If we're going to live in this shelter together, it's best I know yours."

He took the smaller saplings and wove them horizontally through the arched ones. The shelter was starting to look like something substantial.

"Going to be plenty of room for two. Now, all we need to do is fill in the spaces. What do you think? Should we fill them with sod? Or maybe leaves?" Zach waited for an answer.

The boy looked at the structure, "My dad could make one like that," he said.

"I bet it would be better, too," Zach said. "How did you get separated?"

The boy said nothing.

Zach took off his jacket, put it over the boy's shoulders, and said, "I'll be right back."

On the other side of the little creek were some pine trees. Zach gathered as much pine straw as he could and carried it back to the new shelter, scattering it on the ground, making a bed of sorts. Finally, he draped his poncho over the entire structure. "Well, that should keep us dry," Zach said. "We can improve it later. C'mon in, son. Let's get out of this rain."

The boy hesitated, but crawled in, and Zach followed and lay down beside him and put his arms around him. Slowly, the boy's shivering stopped. They lay there in silence.

9

Andersonville Prison– Day 2

ARLY THE NEXT morning, Zach woke. He could smell wood burning, and he heard the voices of fellow prisoners waking up. The rain had mercifully stopped, and he crawled out and stretched. Around him, various groups of men huddled around campfires, trying to fend off the morning chill. Most of the men had plates or pans. Many had dish-like pieces of metal that Zach quickly surmised were canteen halves. He scouted down around the creek again, this time for bits of firewood. Returning to his tent with an armload, he saw the boy was sitting up.

"Bet you could eat a horse," Zach said to the boy.

"Guess so."

"From the looks of everybody out there, the food wagon is coming soon. We'd best get ready."

Zach reached into the tent and pulled out one of the metal sheets he had brought from Richmond. He beat it with a small stone to form an indentation in the middle. "This should do it, if we need some kind of container for our rations," Zach said. He quickly made another.

The front gates finally opened and a wagon full of food came through. Zach collected rations for the boy and himself. Today's consisted of two quarts of meal, two sweet potatoes, and several small pieces of heavily-salted beef. When they returned to their tent, Zach said, "Now remember, boy, this ration has to last until tomorrow. So let's go slow."

The boy stared at the sweet potato. Zach continued, "Take one of those metal sheets over to one of our neighbors and ask for a hot ember to start our fire."

The boy scurried off while Zach cut the wet bark off a piece of wood. When the kid returned with the glowing ember, the fire started easily. Zach asked him to take his canteen down to the creek and fill it with fresh water, cautioning him to be sure to get the water as far upstream as possible. He used a gentle but firm tone, and the boy, probably driven by hunger, readily complied. Zach mixed the water with the meal, turning it into a gruel or paste that became a sort of pancake when cooked.

The two of them shared the pancake and each had half a sweet potato. While the boy was eating, Zach asked him, "Where did you lose your father?"

"Just outside of Richmond," the boy said.

"How did it happen? Were you together?"

"My mother died in 1860 when I was seven. When Dad signed up, he didn't want to leave me home alone, so I signed up with him as a bugler in his company. He was a captain. We were captured at Mine Run, and they took us to Libby Prison, and we nearly starved. We were put on a train for transfer to Camp Oglethorpe in Macon. On the way, my father broke away to find some food. He tried to steal a chicken from a farm near the railroad tracks and an old farmer shot him dead." The boy started to cry and Zach let him. "He was only trying to get something to eat," the boy sobbed. "He wanted a chicken because he knew it was my favorite."

"Your father must have loved you very much."

The boy replied with only a sob.

"This won't be of much help to you, boy, but think of the good times you and your father had. Think of all the positive things he tried to do for you. Maybe, in your grief, you can realize that even though you lost him, you were fortunate to have had him for the time you did. You will always have memories, and nobody can kill those. In that sense, your father lives on. He lives in the things he taught you, in your experiences together."

After a pause, the boy wiped his eyes with his sleeve. "That is exactly what my mother said to me when my kid brother died."

"What's your name? "

"Beau. Short for Beauregard."

"Well, Beau, care to go for a little walk? Let's find out what this place has to offer, if anything."

"Okay."

Their shelter was located near the northeast corner of the stockade, just to the left of the entrance. They strolled to the west, then south along the western side, down the hill until they reached the stream. There, they noticed several very small springs coming up out of the red clay. None of them had much flow, but the water did appear to be pure and clean as it trickled down the bank into the brook. The brook itself flowed west to east, following the slant of the ground. There were twenty- to fifty-foot swampy areas on both sides of the brook that made it difficult to cross to the south side of the stockade. To get across, they followed a walkway made up of a series of steps made of boards, logs, or pieces of stone. They squished in the mud when they were stepped on.

As they crossed, they could see the construction of the remainder of the stacked walls being completed. They could also see the Rebel cannon, aimed menacingly in their direction, cannoneers at the ready. Heading back east along the southern side, they turned to the north and encountered the creek again. The down-current side. This was the area the prisoners used as a latrine, and the odor was sickening. Flies, filth, and muck. The area was impassable to the north, so they doubled back and crossed the brook near where they had the first time, ending up back where they had started. Zach estimated the inside of the stockade was about nine hundred by thirteen hundred feet.

When they got back to their hut, the giant gates opened, and another four or five hundred prisoners entered. The whole process from the day before started all over again. Some of the prisoners who had been there for more than several days rushed up to the newcomers, looking for news.

Zach and Beau spent the rest of the day working to improve their living quarters. That night, as the two of them huddled on the pine straw, keeping each other warm, Zach gave Beau his opinion about their situation. With new prisoners coming in every day, he thought the camp would quickly become overcrowded, taxing what few resources they had. The brook running down the middle of the camp bothered Zach. They were expected to drink and bathe on one end while the other was used for latrines and waste. It was already a cesspool and promised to get a lot worse. Zach suggested that they get their drinking water from the springs whenever possible. He intended to make a funnel from one of his metal sheets to use to fill the water container he was going to make. Zach thought they should make every effort to escape. He had no plan, but had several ideas that might be worth further thought. They talked about being exchanged, but they knew, being so deep into Rebel territory, the chances of that were minimal.

In the middle of the night, Zach awoke with a start. Beau was shaking him. "Wake up, wake up," Beau said.

Zach shook his head trying to clear the cobwebs.

"Cauchemare?" Beau asked.

"Huh?"

"Bad dream?"

"Yes, I guess you could say that. A real bad dream."

Beau fell back to sleep while Zach thought about his recurring dream. The dead man. The picture. Would he ever find her?

IO

Andersonville Prison – Day 27

DAYS STRETCHED TO weeks and the monotony of daily life settled in. The rations had at first, been quite adequate, but it seemed that each day the quality and quantity got worse. A group of fifteen men were caught trying to go over the wall. They were captured on the other side and brought back inside the stockade, each chained to a six-pound ball. The rumor was that over fifty men were involved in the scheme, and that someone from the inside had tipped off the guards.

The next day, a detail of sixteen Negroes entered through the front gate, followed by a man on horseback, carrying a rifle. The Negroes were shirtless, shoeless, and their pants were tattered shreds below their knees. They walked single file with a slow, rhythmic pace, carrying wooden posts. Their heads hung down as each followed the man in front. The foreman ordered them to drive the posts into the ground and showed them where to put them. Slowly and methodically, they drove the posts around the inner perimeter, with each post exactly twenty feet from the walls. At first, the Negroes seemed nervous, but as they settled into a routine, one of them, a tall, slender man, broke into song. He would sing a verse and the rest would chime in with the chorus. At first, Zach could understand the words but not the meaning.

"Well, long John,
He's long gone,
He's long gone,
Mister John, John,

Ol' Big-eye John,
Oh, John, John,
It's a long John."

Watching the slaves, Zach compared his plight to theirs. He decided that even though his conditions were terrible, theirs were worse. They had no hope. He marveled that they sang.

Finally, as the sun set behind ominous clouds in the west, they finished the job and marched out again.

The prisoners were told no one was to cross the line of posts, which quickly became known as the "dead line" because anyone who crossed it was shot.

————

The flapping of the poncho against the top of the shelter woke Zach the next morning. The rain that had fallen in the night had given way to a strong, cold wind that seemed to blow through unobstructed. He got up and decided to brave the chill and go down to the creek to wash. The little spring that he normally used was hardly flowing, so he found another nearer the new "deadline."

He kneeled down, and as he was washing, two men approached, both whispering in hushed voices. Zach could only see their feet. As he looked up at the men, they stepped away, as if they didn't want anyone to hear what they were talking about.

Zach was almost finished when he heard a shot ring out, blood splattered over the ground in front of him, and one of the men fell dead beside him with a bullet hole in the back of his head.

Zach jumped to his feet. The other man stood, looking down at his friend, in shock. Zach looked over at the nearest guard. He was smiling. Zach guessed the dead man had not crossed the "dead line," but the guards had wanted to make a point.

————

Early one April morning, the front gate opened and a rider entered. It was the new commandant of the prison, Captain Henri Wirz, arrived to personally conduct rollcall. Wirz was a short, trim-bearded man. He had a little head, a receding hairline, and his tobacco-stained beard came to a point below his chin. He ordered all the prisoners to form ranks and remain standing at full attention until all were counted, which took a several hours. A few of the men started to fall out before the count was completed and in reprisal, Wirz withheld rations for everyone for the rest of the day. The next day he repeated the exercise. The prisoners were weakened from lack of food. But again, after several hours, some men fell out of line before the count was completed. Wirz ordered rations withheld again. On the third day, the men still struggled to stay in formation, but they somehow managed to satisfy Wirz, and one-day's rations were issued.

Zach and Beau rose well before the sun each morning to go down near the creek, which was now being called "Stockade Branch," where they would get their drinking water for the day. They did their best to get it from one of the springs, but the flow varied each day. As he had promised, Zach had formed one of his metal sheets into a small funnel that allowed them to divert a typically small trickle into Beau's canteen. They would then wash themselves as best they could from the uppermost reaches of the creek. Even though Beau didn't like this part, Zach insisted.

In addition to the prisoners' job of handling their own comfort and shelter, the main topics of conversation were: exchange, escape, and food. Of the three, the only one that anybody could try to do anything about was escape. The stockade walls were so high, and the guards so numerous, the various ideas to escape over the top were usually quickly dismissed. Tunneling under the walls was often discussed, however. Zach had heard men talking about tunneling but he had not been privy to any specific plans. He thought a lot about escape, but his friendship with Beau meant that if he discovered a good way to do it, they would have to make the attempt together.

Early one rainy morning, Beau and Zach walked down to Stockade Branch to do their morning rituals. Two other prisoners were in the area of their spring and they both had bags of dirt, which they were emptying near the water's edge. As Zach filled the canteen with spring water, the two men approached Beau.

"You're the bugler boy whose father was shot. Is that right?" one asked.

"Yes," Beau replied, with some hesitation.

The man lowered his voice to a whisper, "We have started a tunnel, and we need some help."

"Looks like you have plenty of help around here. Why Beau?" asked Zach.

"We need somebody small. We have a tunnel, and when we string it, it's long enough to be way beyond the outer wall, but we don't think we've gone under it yet."

"How deep?"

"About five feet. The walls are sunk five feet, too, so we are confused. We don't want to come to the surface unless we are sure where we are. Wouldn't do us no good if we came up under Wirz's cot," the man said with a grin.

Zach was mildly interested. Maybe this was the way for the two of them to make a run for it. "How will Beau's size help you?"

"We figure we need to go another twenty to thirty feet, and with this young man's size, the hole could be much smaller." He looked at Beau. "With your help, we could bore that extra twenty feet, then come up. If we're in the right spot, we widen the hole and goodbye, we're outta here. All the men in on this are getting impatient, and the longer we wait, the more chance the Johnnies will find us out."

Beau looked up at Zach. "Can I?"

Zach thought for a moment. "How many nights' digging 'til you think Beau would come up?"

"No more than two."

"What will they do if they catch him?"

"Boy this young? Probably nothin'," the man replied. "Even these guys don't mess around with kids. Most of them have kids at home."

"I'm no 'kid,'" said Beau.

"Yep, we know that. But they don't," the man said with another smile.

"How many in on this?" Zach asked.

"Eleven. Thirteen countin' you two."

Beau looked back up at Zach. This time Zach nodded.

"Okay. I'm in," Beau said. "When do I start?"

"My tent is on the upper west side near the deadline. Meet me there just after dark. Not a word to anybody, you hear?"

"Beau will be there," Zach said.

"One more thing," the man said. "Beware of those raiders on the other side of Stockade Branch. They're a bunch of liars and thieves. They will stop at nothing. They will report you to the Rebs for anything just to get better rations and treatment. Give them a wide berth and don't confront them. They're mean and tough."

That evening, Beau and Zach found the man's shelter. His name was Jim Gibbons, and after greeting them, he took them back up the hill a bit to another, larger tent, also located near the deadline. Gibbons took Beau inside and pulled up a piece of oilcloth, revealing a hole in the ground. He gave Beau a metal plate, nothing more than a canteen half, and told him how to dig.

"Crawl in there, and when you get to the end, start digging with this. Are you right handed?"

When Beau replied that he was, Gibbons told him to hold the dish in his right hand to dig. He demonstrated the technique, and had Beau repeat the procedure. "Now, it's blacker than black in there, son. As you crawl in, you will soon know if you can take being closed in. If you get too scared to go on, just back out, and we will find somebody else. Okay?"

Beau took the canteen half and squatted down to enter. "Once you get to the end, start digging. Be careful not to dig up or dig down. Just dig in front of you. When you've dug a pile of lose dirt in front of you, spread it out, and crawl over it, and keep goin'. We will have men behind to remove the excess dirt. You got it?"

"Yep."

"One last thing. No talking."

Before Beau jumped in, he looked back at Zach. Zach nodded, and he scrabbled down the hole. Zach wondered if he had made the right decision as he watched Beau disappear into the ground. If Beau got caught, they might try to make an example of him. Maybe they might exchange him, if he was lucky, or they might send him to another prison, or worst of all, they might hang him.

Four hours later, Beau crawled into their tent. Zach was waiting. Beau told him they had had dug a record of twelve feet. He lay down next to Zach and told him what it felt like being in the narrow tunnel in pitch darkness. The tunnel was just wide enough for him to turn around. Roots from bushes, trees, and plants hung down, and he quickly learned to keep his eyes shut and his mouth closed. He had no idea of how far he had come or how far he had to go. Finally, he'd reached the end and started to dig. With his right hand, he'd swept the canteen half across the dirt in front of him. Each time peeling off a thin layer, feeling the loosened earth falling in piles in front of him. The earth gave way easily to his makeshift shovel, and his progress was steady. As dirt accumulated, he pushed it down the sides of the tunnel. He could hear the breathing of men behind him as they took the dirt and pushed it farther back. He had no idea if he was going up, down, left, or right. He just kept digging.

Several hours later, Zach woke Beau up from a deep sleep. "Let's go down and try to get some of that red dirt off before it gets light," he said. "If one of the guards sees you, they won't have a hard time figuring out what you've been doing."

Zach reached for Beau's canteen, where he hung it on a branch by the doorway. It wasn't there.

He looked around. "Where's your canteen?" he said.

"Haven't seen it since we left to go digging last night," Beau said.

"Bastards. Those goddamned raiders Jim was talking about. Well, it won't be hard to find. Probably the only one in this camp with the 'Third Michigan' insignia."

"You think they just took it?"

"I'll handle this," Zach said. "Don't worry about it."

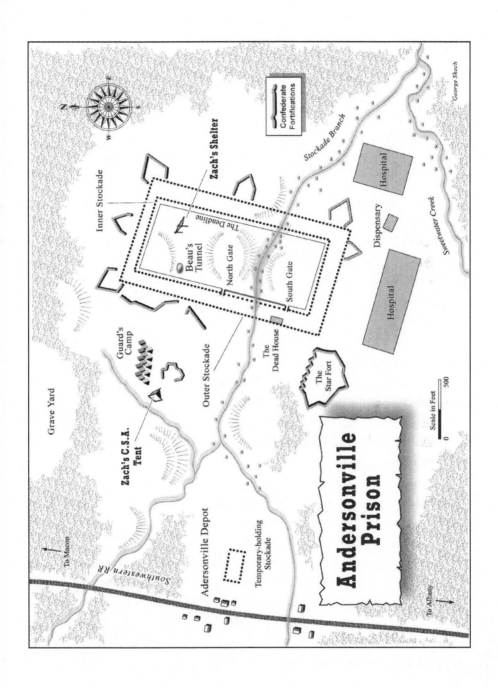

II

Andersonville Prison – Day 32

AFTER RATIONS, ZACH spent the afternoon forming one of his metal sheets. He folded the sheet diagonally, then doubled it over twice, each time pounding the edges flat with a rock. The result was a rudimentary weapon resembling a knife with a very sharp point stiffened by eight layers of metal. Using that same tool, he whittled a handle with a slit on one end into which he inserted his makeshift blade.

Beau had slept most of the afternoon, and when he woke, he saw Zach's weapon. "What are you going to do with that?" he asked.

"A lot of thieving going on around here and by the looks of things those New Yorkers over there are getting entirely out of hand."

"You going to use that thing?"

"Will if I have too. Something has to be done."

"Don't you go over there alone."

"Time for us to walk over to the dig. You ready?"

Jim was waiting for them when they arrived. He instructed Beau to continue as the previous night and leave his half-canteen at the end of the tunnel when he came back, for use by the first escapee when they decided to make the final break, which would probably be the next night. They did not want to wait. The chances of the Johnnies finding out only multiplied with time.

After Beau disappeared into the tunnel, Zach went back to his tent. He waiting several hours until the camp quieted down and the few fires had either gone out or were reduced to amber glows. He put his new knife under his belt and walked toward Stockade Branch.

The prison population was growing at a rapid rate, and with no system of walkways, the shelters were packed densely together, making walking in the dark difficult. He knew exactly where he wanted to go, and as his eyes adapted to the darkness, the ambient light provided enough illumination for him to make his way. He crossed the stream in the area closest to the deadline, where most got their drinking water, and proceeded straight up the hill until he got to the raiders camp. As he weaved his way among the sleeping men, he saw the canteen marked "Third Michigan," brazenly hanging on a tent pole, as if the thief was daring someone to do something about it.

Zach squatted down to crawl into the tent. The man was sleeping with his feet toward the open end. Zach pulled out the knife with his left hand, and with his right fist, hit him as hard as he could, swinging upward at the man's jaw. With a crunching sound, the man's jaw either broke or dislocated. With his hand over the man's mouth, he whispered, "One sound and you're dead."

The man's eyes opened in terror. Zach transferred his weapon to his right hand, and with his left hand on the thief's mouth, he cut a slash across his forehead. Then he swung his fist and hit the man's jaw in the same place as he had before, crawled out of the tent, grabbed the canteen, and disappeared into the night.

Zach had waited for several hours when Beau finally returned.. Entering the shelter, he was smiling. "We go tomorrow night," he whispered, excitement in his voice.

"Good work. Now we should be thinking about how to escape the hounds once they get on our trail. You have any experience with bloodhounds?"

Beau lay down on his blanket. "I used to go coon hunting with coon dogs."

"These bloodhounds have keener senses of smell than even coon hounds do. When we break out, we need to stay with the group for a short while, then split from them and hope the dogs follow the pack instead of us. We can work downstream and find deeper water. Can you swim?"

"Yes, Michigan is full of lakes."

They talked and planned late into the night, waking up with the sunrise. When they crawled out of the tent to stretch, they saw the front gate open and

Captain Wirz ride in, followed by two sergeants. He had not made an appearance since the infamous rollcall, and he knew he was not welcome.

"Zach Harkin?" Wirz called out. "Zach Harkin, front and center!"

The first thought that ran through Zach's mind was the raiders had somehow found him out and told Wirz about it. Then he thought that they had finally found out who he was, and they were going to hang him for what he did at Shiloh. Maybe they wanted him for beating up the captain back in Bristol.

"Zach Harkin?" The captain yelled louder.

Zach was only about fifty feet away. He had no choice but to raise his hand to present himself.

"You Zach Harkin?" Wirz said.

When Zach nodded, Wirz continued, "Come with me."

In front of his office, he dismounted and signaled for Zach to follow. He ordered Zach to sit. He was actually punier than he had previously appeared, and he spoke with a staccato German accent. His tone was authoritarian. "How is our sharpshooting friend doing?"

Zach did not answer.

"How is our sharpshooting friend doing?" he asked in a louder, more demanding voice.

"As well as can be expected," Zach muttered.

"Good. That's good to hear." Wirz was silent for a moment then said, "The prisoners seem not to be happy. Maybe because it is so crowded?"

Zach stared at him blankly.

"Are our northern friends planning to escape? Trying to fool my guards?"

Zach felt trapped.

Wirz rose from his chair, leaned over him, and demanded, "Are you planning an escape?"

Wirz stood in front of Zach, no more than two feet away. He tapped his fingers on the desktop in progression, like an impatient teacher.

Zach could not hold Wirz's glare. He looked down and said softly, "I am not involved in any escape attempt."

"Aha, yes. But you know of some. Is that correct?" Wirz's voice was getting higher and his face was turning red. "Is that correct?"

"Sir, those men out there only talk about three things: food, exchange, and escape. They have nothing else to occupy themselves with," Zach said firmly.

Wirz sat down, apparently satisfied. "I suppose you're right." Looking down at a sheet of paper, he continued, "You reported when you first became our guest that you are a gunsmith. Is that correct?"

"Yes sir."

"You are a bit young to be a gunsmith, wouldn't you say?"

"My father has a gun shop in Tennessee. I have been working with him for quite a while."

"I see. Does he have a specialty?"

"He likes to improve guns. Make them more accurate at longer distances with faster actions."

"Mostly American guns, would you say?"

"No, my father is from England. He is equally comfortable with European and U.S. made firearms."

"As well as you, I presume?"

"Well, yes."

"Let me give you a little test." Wirz got up and retrieved a rifle from the corner of the office. It was wrapped in an oilskin. Wirz unsheathed it with care.

Gently laying the rifle on his desk in front of Zach, he continued, "Ever see one of these?"

Zach didn't recognize it. He looked at the butt end of the barrel and saw the name "Mauser," a German manufacturer. The stock was unadorned maple with a dark-stained finish. It was in very good condition and probably had not been used much. Its unique characteristic was a lever mounted on the right side that evidently opened and closed the firing chamber. Zach remembered his father talking about this peculiar kind of ejection mechanism.

"Do you mind?" Zach asked.

"Please."

Zach picked it up and inspected it more closely. While it was obviously a well-made gun, he didn't like the balance. He didn't want to shoulder it, since Wirz might take that as a threat, so he pulled back on the little lever and looked in at the firing pin. And it all came to him. The pin was almost needle shaped instead of the normal, blunter type used in American guns.

"This gun is a Chassepot converted Mauser. Originally a muzzle-loader, converted to a breech-loader. This bolt is a new design used to open the breech, eject a spent cartridge, and insert a new one as the bolt is closed. Very nice," he said, although he was not impressed in the least.

Wirz smiled. "We have just one small problem," Wirz said. "The gun will not fire every time. It only fires some of the time. Do you think you can fix it?"

Zach slid the lever back and looked at the narrow firing pin again. "When the gun misfires, what happens to the cartridge?"

"What do you mean?"

"Do you have a cartridge that misfired?"

"Why, yes. Right here."

Zach looked at the cartridge and immediately knew what the problem was. The firing pin was too sharp. When the pin hit the cartridge, instead of causing percussion, it penetrated the metal, causing it not to fire. The problem would be simple to fix. All he had to do was file the point of the pin down slightly.

Wirz watched Zach hopefully. Zach scratched his head as if in deep thought. "I'm not sure, but I think I can fix it. Might take a little time, though."

"How long?"

"Two or three days, maybe. I'll have to take it apart and rebuild it. Should work fine when I'm done."

"Good. You will start tomorrow. The guard will come at first light. You will receive double rations while you work. If your repair is successful, you will get double rations for an additional two weeks." Wirz got up to call the guard.

"Sir, I want to ask a favor," Zach said. "There is a young boy inside the prison. His name is Beau Andrews, from Michigan, and he is only twelve years old. His father was killed on the train down here and…"

"Yes, I am familiar with the case. His father was a captain and was shot for stealing. Am I right?"

"His son was starving. You can't fault a father for that, can you?"

"Stealing is stealing," Wirz said. He looked down at his beloved gun and back at Zach. "What would you have me do? Turn him loose?"

"Yes. With a note from you he can travel back to Michigan and maybe live with his grandparents."

After a long pause, Wirz said, "You fix my Mauser, and I will see what I can do." He instructed the guard to give Zach a double ration and escort him back to the prison.

12

Andersonville Prison – Day 33

SOMETHING WAS OBVIOUSLY wrong when he returned. Several of the front poles that supported the tent had been smashed, and Beau was missing. Their blankets were strewn around their campsite, and Beau's canteen was gone. His homemade knife was still hidden between the small saplings that held up the back of the tent.

He put the knife in his rear pocket and ran over to Jim's tent.

"They got Beau," Zach yelled to Jim and several of his friends. "I'm going up there and get him."

"Whoa! Hold on a minute, Zach," Jim said. "You can't just expect them to hand him over. They'll kill you and Beau, too. If they haven't already." Jim's voice lowered to a whisper. "Look, we're making our move tonight. Everything is ready. Can't wait another night. If you go up there and raise hell, the guards will be alerted and our chances of an escape will go down the creek. Let's think this through. Why do you think they took Beau?"

"Could be because I beat the hell out of the guy who stole his canteen last night, and gave him a special reminder that he'll see every morning in the mirror from now on."

"Holy Christ. That wasn't very smart. You've stirred up a real big hornet's nest."

"That may be, but I'm going up there to get Beau. You can stay or come along as you wish." Zach stood. His face was red.

"Don't go. You'll ruin everything," Jim said.

"If they hurt Beau, I'll kill them all." Zach ran toward the creek. He jumped across. When he got near the tent where he had been the night before, he saw it was surrounded by at least a dozen men, all looking angry, with their sleeves rolled up. One of them held Beau, who shook his head at Zach in warning. Sitting on the ground amongst them, his jaw wrapped in blood-soaked rags, was the man who had stolen Beau's canteen. The gash on his forehead was covered with a blood-soaked rag.

Zach froze.

The apparent leader of the group held the canteen up in the air. "Looking for something?" He waved the canteen in Zach's direction. "Well, here it is," he threw the canteen just beyond the deadline.

The man holding Beau turned him loose and he immediately ran to retrieve the canteen.

"No, Beau! No!" Zach shouted.

Beau crossed the deadline, and two rifle shots rang out, and two bullets ripped into Beau. One through his chest and another through his forehead, exiting the back of his head, spewing blood and bone fragments. Beau was dead before he hit the ground.

Zach turned his gaze from his dead friend back to the men standing in front of the tent.

"Now, how would you like to come over here and apologize to this man," the leader said, pointing to the robber with the gash on his forehead.

Zach looked back at the boy's crumpled body, then turned his gaze to the leader. He pulled his homemade knife and charged. He caught glimpses of others in the group, wielding clubs. On he came with a roar, and the clubs rained down on his head, shoulders, and arms. His momentum carried him head first into the leader. He thrust his knife into the man's soft belly with an upward motion, just as the man, who had a real knife, slashed at him, opening a deep wound from his hairline to his chin. Zach's knife blow lifted the man off his feet and he went down with a gurgling sound as air bubbled out of the hole in his chest. Then something hit Zach hard on the head and he buckled to the ground.

13

S OFT RAIN PATTERED on the tin roof of the gun shop. Zach went for another cup of coffee. He stood by the stove and looked out the window, staring into space. After a pause, he returned to his seat.

"I guess they threw me into Stockade Branch to die. Almost did, too, but Jim and his men pulled me out. They got the guards to take me to the hospital outside the gates," Zach said.

"Was Captain Wirz looking out after you?" Chris asked.

"Yeah, guess he really wanted his Mauser fixed. The gun wasn't really anything much. I never did know exactly why he prized it so."

"Was Wirz as bad as everybody thinks?" Chris asked. "I mean the guy was the only Confederate hanged for war crimes; he ordered the creation of the deadline. Quite a few soldiers were shot in cold blood if they so much as got close to that line. Seems like that in itself was a war crime of the highest order."

"They shot Beau. At the time, I could have ripped the arms and legs off those two guards. You know, one of them was only fifteen. Lee called for all the able regular army soldiers, and they were replaced with kids and old men. All of them were trying to prove how tough they were."

"But they were just following Wirz's orders, right?" Chris said. "I mean you can't really blame the guards."

"Initially, I blamed the guards and Wirz," Zach said. "Beau didn't have a chance. Then, after I thought about it, I could only blame myself. The idea of a 'deadline' did not originate with Wirz. Some of our own prisons, such as the federal Camp Douglas, had deadlines, too. Thinking about it objectively, a deadline was an effective way to discourage escapes."

Chris wondered if his employer was ready for any kind of partial exoneration of Wirz. The hatred and bitterness were still very much alive.

"How could you possibly blame yourself?" Chris asked. "You had nothing to do with it."

"Oh, yes I did. When I went back to get the canteen the first time, I should have known they would figure it all out and try to get back at me for what I did. It was foolhardy. That, and I wasn't there to protect Beau when they came. I can never forgive myself for that."

"You're being pretty tough on yourself." Then, changing the subject, Chris said, "So, that's how you got the scar on your face."

Zach ran his finger over the scar, "Yep. Just missed my eye. Lucky it healed."

"You must have thought a lot about ways to escape," Chris said.

Zach took a deep breath and slowly exhaled, the pain registering on his face. "Yep. We talked about all kinds of ways: tunneling, sneaking out when the gates were open, overpowering the guards when they fed us. Some of the prisoners tried to sneak away when they were outside the gates, collecting wood or on some other special duty, but the one method that seemed to be most likely to succeed was just storming the gates. Many of the men were not strong enough to participate, but there were well over ten thousand who were, and if we had all charged at once, we could have overwhelmed the guards. I guess we just didn't have the right leadership to get it done."

"What happened to Beau's tunnel?" Chris asked.

For the first time, Zach smiled. "Oh, that goddamned tunnel. You know, when they measured how long it was, it should have come out almost a hundred feet beyond the outer wall. We figured we hadn't tunneled under it because those vertical logs were buried at least five feet in the ground, and our tunnel was about five feet deep, and we never saw them. It was a big mystery. Until one night, when one of the guys felt something move underneath his tent, and when he tried to crawl out, he fell into a big hole. He screamed, thinking he was being called by the devil, 'til some friends pulled him out."

"So?"

"It was Beau's tunnel! Evidently, everybody who'd helped dig the tunnel was right-handed, and when they dug with the canteen halves, they would sweep across in front of them and each time, the tunnel would veer a little to the left. It was the damnedest thing. The tunnel just made a big circle, ending up only twenty feet or so from where it started. After the initial disappointment, it became a big joke. It was something everybody could laugh about."

Zach looked out the window at a blue jay that had lit on a tree limb. The bird flew away, but Zach continued to stare. "Poor Beau," he said. "I'd still give anything to see his face if he would have found out the tunnel was a goddamned circle."

A customer came into the shop and Chris said he would return in the morning. Back in his room, Chris began writing his next submission. He knew the episode with Zach attacking Beau's captors would make great copy, with the u-shaped tunnel adding some humor, but he sensed that the bigger story had to do with Wirz.

14

Andersonville Prison – Day 34

Sometime later, Zach opened his eyes. The sun was shining through the fabric of the tent he lay in, and something was written on it that he didn't understand. He realized he could see out of only his right eye, the other being covered. He took a breath and winced from the pain in his ribs. The air was different. The foul latrine odor was gone. Still not knowing where he was, Zach ran his hand over the left side of his face. It was all bandaged. His face throbbed. He looked down and saw he was covered with a sheet. A clean sheet. He heard voices outside. Happy voices.

Next to him was a man on a cot with his leg heavily bandaged. He wore a Rebel campaign cap.

Zach looked up at the letters on the fabric again, and it occurred to him he was seeing the letters "CSA" from the inside. He was in a Confederate hospital tent.

The Rebel beside Zach sneered at him and whispered, "If Captain Wirz wasn't stopping in every couple of hours, checking on you, I would personally help you see your maker. Even with this mangled leg, you egg-sucking Yankee son-of-a-bitch. You killed my father and two brothers. You burnt my home, destroyed my farm. Your kind ruined everything I have. Mark my words, if you stay here long, regardless of Wirz, you're a dead man."

Zach could see the fury in the man's bloodshot eyes. His unkempt beard was matted with red dirt. His face was gray, and dark circles ringed his eyes. His campaign cap was worn, the hand stitched CSA on the front, frazzled and frayed. He was a soldier who had plainly seen the horrors of war, realized his side might lose, and knew his life was forever changed. Zach could relate. Although his experience had been different, his life also had been unalterably changed. He felt only pity, remorse, and deep sorrow for the man beside him.

An hour later, a white-frocked surgeon entered the tent. "I'm Doctor W.H. Credille," he said. "Most just call me Bill the Doc. Captain Wirz wants to see you as soon as possible. How are you doing?"

The man in the next cot swore.

"Doing okay, I guess. Where am I?"

"You're in Sumter Hospital. Guess you could say you're a guest of Jeff Davis," the doctor said. "We have cases of smallpox with some of the new inmates, so the colonel insisted we put you here."

The surgeon gave a cursory glance to Zach's head bandages, but was more interested in his ribs and abdomen. He probed with his hands, pressing different areas, watching Zach's face to see if he winced. "Any pain here?" he asked.

"Just pretty sore all over, Doc."

"Well, you look good enough to go. I'll tell Wirz you can be discharged in the morning. Meantime, rest up. You'll need it." He tapped Zach's foot and walked over to the other man.

"How's the leg today, Corporal?" he asked.

The corporal just scowled. "Goddamned Yankee. Why did you see him first? Doesn't the fact that I am a member of the Confederate Army and he's a no good-son-of-a-bitch Yankee mean anything to you? Where are your priorities? Don't you care?"

An increasing breeze wafted the tent canvas; the air was thick with the possibility of rain.

The surgeon bent to look at the wounded soldier's leg. He smiled. "Feeling better, I see. Back to your old ornery disposition." He unwrapped the soldier's bloodstained bandages. When the wound was uncovered, a vile stench emanated. "Looks like the leg will have to go, soldier. I might be able to save your knee. Not sure. But you have gangrene all the way up to it."

The soldier glowered.

"We'll take care of it right now," the doctor said. "I'll call for a stretcher."

"Like hell you will! There's nothing wrong with this leg." The man turned on his cot and tried to get up. His leg gave out and he collapsed on the floor. He pleaded, "Please Doc, not my leg."

Two men came in and carried him out. He spat as they passed Zach. "May God personally see you to the gates of hell," he said. "And all the rest of you Yankee sons-of-bitches."

A few minutes later Zach heard a long, horrifying scream.

Alone, Zach got up and peered out of the tent to see exactly where he was in relation to the prison walls. Heavy clouds had gathered, blocking the setting sun. He was on a high ridge that looked down into the prison from the southwest. He could see the train depot, where he had arrived a few very long weeks ago. The tracks passed within a hundred yards of where he stood. To his immediate right were sheds, where he assumed the guards bunked. Far to his right was a large group of makeshift temporary shelters that Zach was later to learn was the new prisoner hospital. Looking down into the prison itself, he could see Stockade Branch meandering from just to the right of the train depot down into the prison and exiting to the east. To the north, across Stockade Branch and halfway up the far hill, he could see a fenced enclosure holding the bloodhounds the guards used to chase down escapees.

As a boy, Zach had used coonhounds to hunt raccoons at night. He had been impressed then by the sensitivity of their sense of smell. They could follow the scent of their prey with ease, and when they got close, they would chase with their heads up, following an invisible scent trail. He had heard that bloodhounds had a much better sense of smell than even coonhounds had.

Far to the west, lightning lit up the gathering clouds, and the air went still. To the north, the smoke from an approaching train rose above the trees. Probably another big load of prisoners, Zach thought, going back into the tent. He lay down, and for the first time in several days, he thought about the man he had killed, and his family. He thought about Abbeville. He remembered his school geography class: maps showing South Carolina as north of Georgia somewhere.

He had to get there. He could not stay in this godforsaken prison. His chances of escape were much better now than they would ever be from inside the walls. Now was the time to escape. But how to evade the hounds? A plan began to take shape in his mind.

15

Andersonville Prison – Day 35

IN THE MORNING, Zach awoke to the earthy sound of a steady, cool rain and the smell of cooking fire smoke from the officer's mess tent nearby. A soft breeze from the east suggested the rain might last all day. He lay on his cot and mulled over the fledgling plan he had formulated the night before. He went over each step again and again, trying to guess what might go wrong at each juncture, and then figuring out different options from there. His experience working in his father's gun shop helped him. Whether the task was making a new gun or repairing an old one, his father would always meticulously make a plan from beginning to end, trying to cover all contingencies. The rain falling outside was one such contingency.

A guard brought Zach to Wirz's office.

"Heard you were involved in some trouble the other night," Captain Wirz said. "You ready to go to work? Sorry I couldn't help your friend."

"I'll be able to fix your gun," Zach said. His voice was expressionless. I will need a couple tools and a piece of sheet metal."

"You must be a pretty tough guy. That man you killed was bigger than you." Wirz said.

"A ball peen hammer and a piece of sheet metal," Zach restated.

"You go back inside those walls and you might not come out," Wirz said.

"A rasp file, too. The sheet metal should be about a foot square. A little peach tree gum, and that should do it," Zach said. "Where will I work?"

"Peach tree gum?"

"We use it sometimes to make a seal. You have a couple peach trees just outside. Where will I work?" Zach said.

"How long did you say it would take you?" Wirz asked.

Zach replied that it would be three days or more.

"You'll work right here in my office, where we can keep an eye on you," Wirz said. "Wouldn't look good on my record if a prisoner escaped with my own rifle."

Zach couldn't tell if Wirz was kidding or not. "And the tools?" he asked.

Wirz didn't answer. He was looking at his rifle as a father might watch his sleeping child.

"Well, you might be right," Zach said. "Those raiders are a tough bunch. And they are not afraid to gang up on anybody. They know no rules." The rain had gotten stronger, beating on the top of the tent, making it difficult to hear. "Yep, I won't get much sleep when I go back. They could come at me for revenge any time, night or day."

"I think you will stay where you were in the guard hospital until you finish," Wirz announced.

"So I fix your rifle and then you send me back in to get killed, is that right, sir?"

Wirz's eyes shifted from his rifle over to Zach, then back. "We could try some other arrangements."

Zach figured he had pushed as hard as he dared, plus he had accomplished exactly what he had wanted.

After Wirz had set Zach up with the tools he asked for on a small table next to his desk, Zach proceeded to take the rifle apart. While he could have made the repairs without tearing it down, he was buying time.

The Mauser was truly unique, but even though Zach had never seen one before, he understood how it worked. The key to the design was the ejector, which ejected a spent cartridge when the bolt was unlocked and pulled back. Then a spring mechanism pushed a new cartridge into the empty chamber as the bolt was closed. Between shots, the shooter did not have to take his eyes off his target. The design was simple and probably reliable.

Wirz watched over Zach's shoulder. "What is wrong with it?" he asked.

"Nothing I can't fix," Zach replied. "Just give me a couple days and it will be better than new."

Wirz seemed satisfied. "I will attend my duties," he said. "Remember, my guard is posted just outside the door, in case you get any ideas. You understand?"

"Where would I go? You have this place locked up tighter than a noose," Zach replied. "Oh, by the way, I will need an unspent cartridge when I reassemble this. Can you arrange that?"

"Wirz's eyes widened. He seemed to understand that Zach would need one, but at the same time he understood the risk. "Yes, of course," he said. "But I will be the one who tests it."

"Understood."

Wirz pivoted and walked out into the rain, his shoes sloshing through the mud.

The rain continued to fall. Zach was sure Stockade Branch would be flowing freely.

Zach had the room to himself. The guard was just outside the door under a small porch roof. Zach took the piece of metal sheet and formed a tube of it with his hands. He wanted the diameter of the tube to be no more than an inch so he used the bolt of the rifle and the ball peen hammer to make it smaller. His tapping caused the guard to look in, but he seemed satisfied with what he saw. Zach took his time. He knew the tube had to be just right. When he finished forming the tube, he stepped outside, and with the guard watching, he scraped some gum off a nearby peach tree, which he used to seal the edges of the tube, making it airtight.

The rain let up somewhat in the middle of the afternoon and another guard came into the office with Zach's double rations. To his surprise, the ration included a warm cup of thick soup with beans and small bits of bacon. He tipped the cup and held the first swallow of liquid in his mouth, savoring the texture and flavor. Salt had been totally absent from his diet during his captivity, and the salted bacon awakened long-dormant taste buds. The meal also included two pieces of hardtack, which Zach soaked in the soup. The usual weevils were missing, and it tasted like it may have been made the day before. He felt a pang of guilt that he was eating such a comparatively robust meal when those inside where eating very little, and what they did get was frequently rancid and bug eaten. The guilt did not last long, however, as he contemplated what he was going to do over the next several days.

The rain got even heavier and thunder rumbled to the west. Wirz came rushing in, breathless, having run from the train depot, followed by two soldiers who only wore partial uniforms. Wirz was wet and angry.

"How am I expected to feed ten thousand prisoners with nothing?" he shouted. "Your Captain Winder must think I'm Jesus Christ—pulling fish and bread out of the air!" Water dripped off the bill of his campaign cap, and off his beard, each time his chin moved. Wirz shook his head and the water fell off his beard and hat and Zach was reminded of a dog shaking its body after coming out of the water.

The two soldiers stood, saying nothing. Wirz was far from finished. "If those prisoners ever united and tried to break out en masse they would certainly succeed." He glanced over at Zach as if only now noticing him sitting there, then as if his presence meant nothing, continued. "Imagine ten thousand men busting through those gates all at once. We could not stop them. They would arm themselves and start marauding the countryside, destroying everything. Every day we don't feed them, the chances increase and you, Winder, and all the rest of you would bear the blame."

Neither of the two soldiers seemed to be taking Wirz's rants very seriously. Zach detected a faint smirk on one man's face.

"Sir, with all due respect," the smirking man said, "those men in there are too weak and disorganized to do any such thing. Granted they must be hungry, but would they revolt? Not likely. And if they did, our cannons would cut them to shreds with scatter loads."

"Let me tell you something," Wirz retorted. "I know that I am only responsible for the prisoners. You do not answer to me, the guards do not answer to me except when they are inside the walls, and I have no authority over the hospitals. I have very little authority, but this war probably won't last much longer. Lee is just barely able to avoid being taken down by an army twice his size. When this war ends, somebody is going to ask some questions. Questions like, 'why were five hundred or more prisoners being buried a day here?' It would be easy for them to figure out that they were starved to death. Now, let me ask you another question, 'Who do you think they will blame? Who was in charge of providing the food? Who bears this blame?'" He let the weight of his questions sink in. "The answer is, you! You and all the Quartermaster Corps. The whole goddamned lot of you! I can see it all clearly. The lot of you swinging high and dry from a goddamned noose!"

Wirz's face was fiery red. His right eyelid twitched. He took several deep breaths then told the two soldiers to get out, which they did with solemn faces. No more smirks. He wheeled around and sat down at his desk. He buried his head in his hands.

After some time, he looked over at Zach. "Not a word from you to any of your buddies inside about what you just heard. You understand me?"

"Yes, I do," Zach said. He had not known that Wirz had so little authority. He briefly felt compassion for the little man, but he also realized Wirz would never let him go back inside the walls after hearing the conversation that had just taken place.

"Go back to your tent," Wirz said. "Will you be done by tomorrow?"

"Close, but almost surely the day after," Zach said.

A guard took him back to his tent through the pouring rain.

Zach's feet had dried out during the day, but the familiar feel of soaked shoes returned after a few steps. The rain was too heavy for the guard to stand outside, so he told Zach he would be watching from the tent next to his, which opened in the same direction. The guard wore a long white beard and appeared to be nearly sixty years old. He walked with a gimpy leg, and with each step, his right foot swung out, dragging the toe of his shoe in the mud.

The inside of Zach's tent was redolent of the damp, dingy smell of old blankets. The tent was set up on a slight incline and a shallow trench had been dug around the edges, but water still soaked the entire floor. Zach's feet almost slid out from under him as he walked to his cot. Everything was wet: the air, the ground, his clothes, and his feet.

He reached into his back pocket for the logbook. It, too, was wet, but the photo was still dry. The woman. Was she in the Abbeville area? Would anybody recognize her picture? How would he get there? He ripped a slit part way up the rear of the tent, removed a small square of material, and carefully wrapped the book, to make it as waterproof as possible, then he tucked it back into his rear pocket, along with the tube he had made in Wirz's office. He waited for the train to arrive with more prisoners.

16

Andersonville Prison —-Day 35 Late Evening

Despite the din of the heavy rain on the tent, Zach heard the high-pitched screech of the locomotive's brakes. He looked out the front flap. The guard was awake, staring directly at him in the early evening light. The prisoners would be unloaded, then marched the mile or so to the camp. He calculated twenty minutes to unload and fifteen minutes to reach the camp. They would be wet and miserable. Little did they know things would get much worse, Zach thought. They would have to spend the night in the open, on the muddy ground: no shelter, no food, and no room to so much as lie down.

He waited. The smoke from the engine mixed with the earthen muskiness of the mud. Zach heard the guards shouting orders to the prisoners, and knew it was time. He gave the guard one last glimpse of him, then scurried through the back flap, and ran hard toward the train. He stayed off the trail that led from the depot to the camp, dodging the thin pines. The ground was spongy with rain-soaked pine needles, but he was able to make good time. He heard the guards shouting, much closer, to his left as he neared the train. He stopped and crouched by a large tree to catch his breath. He was surprised how his lack of good food and inactivity had changed him. Only a few months before, this little run would have been much easier. Very little light penetrated the woods, and Zach had to rely on sound as he crept toward the train.

The voices got louder, and Zach could hear the sloshing of the prisoner's feet on their trek to the camp. Then they came into view. Tightly packed, lined up two by two. They had their heads down as if careful not to step on the heels of the soldier in front. On they came, like a serpent snaking through the trees, with guards every hundred feet or so. Must be a thousand of them, Zach thought. Considering the way they had packed the prisoners in when he had made the journey, he estimated the train must have at least ten cars. That was good.

Zach moved to within sight of the train. The first and last car were covered. All the rest were open flat cars. The train was headed south, as usual. Two men were in the cab of the engine, one throwing wood into the boiler to build up steam while the other man watched for a signal from the guards.

Finally, a shout, then a wave by the engineer as he pushed forward the throttle lever and the train started to inch forward. The engine was old and worn, and the rail cars looked ready to fall apart. Boards were missing, and the wheels squealed as if pleading for a drop of oil. Zach could not be sure the covered rail cars were empty. He decided he would have to ride a flatcar, weather the rain, and risk being seen. On the other hand, he would be able to escape the train quickly if he had to.

The last car rattled by, and Zach moved. He burst out of the trees alongside the train, passed the rear boxcar, and leapt onto the last flatbed. A shot rang out, and a man shouting "Stop! Stop, Runaway!" Another shot and more shouting. Zach froze, lying flat on the floor of the car. He felt the wet boards through his clothing as he tried to make himself disappear.

The train didn't stop. It continued picking up speed. The engineer probably couldn't hear the shots through the roar of the rain.

The damp wood feeding the engine decreased the train's speed. Zach was afraid they weren't going as fast as a good horse could run. Bloodhounds could certainly run as fast. The train wasn't his ticket to freedom. He would have to jump sometime soon. The more distance between him and the prison the better, he reasoned. He would wait for the best opportunity, but he had no idea what that would be. The rain beat down on his head. He thought about the night he left home, his warm, soft bed. He even thought about the dry tent he had just left. A cold shiver went through his body as he thought about what Wirz would do if he was captured. Surely, Wirz would be embarrassed that a prisoner had escaped from right under his nose. He would have to make an example of him. That probably meant a rope. Zach realized that his shivers were not caused by wet and cold. He was scared.

A bolt of lightning lit up the dark sky as the train crossed a swollen stream, lapping at the bottom of the railroad bridge. *A couple more hours of this rain and the bridge will be gone*, he thought. The car jolted to the left and right and up and down, moving with the uneven rails.

He looked back and saw movement. Then he heard the whoop of a bloodhound. The hound was running alongside of the boxcar, directly toward Zach, closing quickly. Zach crouched, ready to leap. Then the brakes screamed as the train came to an unexpected stop, throwing Zach forward. The hound was just below him, howling like he'd treed a 'coon. Zach ran forward, jumping from flatbed to flatbed with the hound snarling just a few feet below. Through the rain, Zach saw the train had stopped because of a washed out bridge. Reaching the first boxcar, he crossed to the other side, jumped off, and ran toward the front of the train. The hound ran under the car and overtook Zach, its jaws clamping hard on his leg.

Zach saw the swollen stream just ahead. He grabbed the hound, but could not loosen its grip. The dog's legs were held out straight in front of him, as if he were the rope in a tug of war. Just a few more feet, and Zach could jump. He reached down, clutched the animal by its scruff, and picked it up. The hound still hung on, but Zach was able to move the last few steps and jump off the bridge embankment into the churning black water. Airborne, he felt the dog release its grip.

His momentum carried him deep into the roiling water and pushed him downstream. He kicked hard, propelling himself with his hands and arms. Everything was black. He had no idea which way was up or down. Something big brushed his side. A large pine tree, rolling as it shot forward. But what was forward? He tried to steady himself in the water, to let his buoyancy carry him to the surface, feeling heavy as the water fought his every move. His foot touched the muddy bottom. His lungs were ready to burst. He was thrust along until he hit a boulder. He glanced off, and again was moving, bouncing along the bottom. In a frantic effort to find the surface, he planted his feet in the rocks and silt, and pushed. Beyond his capacity to hold his breath, he grabbed a tree limb, pulled down hard, and exhaled just as his head broke the surface. He tasted the sweetness of air and tried to orient himself.

The stream flattened out and the current slowed. He stroked to one side, hoping to find the water's edge, still unable to see. He was losing strength. His kick had no power. Logs, brush, and flotsam blocked his progress as he fought for the safety of firm ground. He rolled over on his back to conserve his strength. His head hit a tree in a pinewood that had been inundated by the flood. He grabbed it and hung on. He tried to stand, and to his surprise, he found he was only in two feet of water.

Zach slogged through the woods, going tree to tree in the dim light. The water slowly became shallower, and at last his feet emerged on solid ground. The rain had stopped. He sat down, unable to take another step, and fell into a death-like sleep.

Zach woke with a start. Dawn light filtered into the dark, dank woods. He looked up through the trees and saw clear sky. He felt his wet clothes still clinging to his skin, and the early morning chill made him shiver. He stood. The swollen stream had receded, leaving brown slime that covered the pine needles in a thin blanket. Something was wrong. Something had awakened him. Then he heard the distinctive baying of bloodhounds. He had heard them several times back in Knoxville, and always pitied whatever poor slave they were after. His or her chances of getting away were minuscule, and when caught, the discipline would be swift, brutal, and possibly lethal.

The hounds bore down on him, and he took off at a full run, heading back toward the stream. His shoes slipped in the muddy residue and he used the trees to keep his balance. When he reached the still-swollen stream, he could hear the baying of the hounds change to a whoop that meant they had passed the spot where he had slept and they could probably see him. He did not take the time to look back.

He hit the water and swam toward the middle of the stream. He knew bloodhounds could pick up a man's scent from the air if they were close enough. The current in the deepest part of the stream was still very strong. He glanced toward the water's edge and saw the hounds jumping into the water, swimming toward him.

Zach dug into his pocket and pulled out the metal tube. He rolled over onto his back, inserted the tube into his mouth, and floated downstream that way, his head submerged. Moving with the current, feet first. He stayed under the water as much as he could, keeping in the faster current. Occasionally, he raised his head to be sure he was tracking the middle of the current. Then he would submerge again. Sometime later, he raised his head and listened for the dogs. He heard nothing.

Zach felt safer with each seeming mile. The water was red and turbid, with visibility less than three or four inches. He raised his head to steer himself with his arms as the stream took a sharp right turn. As he rounded the corner, he saw a bridge ahead. It was crowded with men looking upstream. Men with dogs. He took several deep breaths and dove to the bottom, his tube in his hand. The current was still fast, and he swam downward, feeling for the bottom. The water seemed about five feet deep. He moved with easy strokes to conserve his breath. He swam until his lungs were ready to burst, then inserted the tube, turned over, and slowly came to the surface. He blew on the tube, but he wasn't there yet. He tried again with the same result. On the third try, the tube cleared, and he took a few deep breaths, and without looking, he submerged again.

Using this method, he swam on, and by late afternoon, the stream merged with a much bigger river, headed to the southeast. Even though he had been floating for most of the journey, he felt weak. Using a crawl stroke, he swam to the left bank and pulled himself up. His legs were shaky, his strength depleted. He collapsed, feeling the warmth of the setting sun. He would have to eat tomorrow, he thought, then he slept.

He awoke the next morning, shivering. The sun cast shadows through the trees onto a slick layer of silt left by the receding water. With his muscles protesting, Zach trudged off through the pine forest, away from the river, toward the rising sun. He checked the leg that had been bitten by the bloodhound. The wound was swollen and red, but appeared not to be serious.

He was hungry. He remembered his father using the expression "I could eat the bark off a tree" and now he understood what it meant. He picked a piece of fungus off the side of a tree. It could be food or it could be poison. He stuck the piece in his pocket anyway, in case he had to take the chance.

The pines thinned, yielding to a large expanse of open field bordered by a crude wooden fence in poor repair. Cotton waved in the breeze, in full bloom. He followed the fence line until he reached a meadow that was fenced off from the cotton field. On the far side of the meadow, several cows grazed, their tails swishing at flies and their udders swollen with milk. Zach's mouth watered at the thought of the warm liquid soothing the pangs in his stomach. The fence line made a right turn, leading to two small sheds and a broken-down house. Between the sheds was a garden with two people tending it, their backs just showing above a row of young corn.

Zach climbed over the fence and a short distance from the two workers, he said, "Hello."

Two dark faces looked his way. They appeared to be man and wife, and both looked startled as they straightened to greet him. The man's eyes darted from Zach to the trees beyond. The woman looked back at the house. They seemed frightened.

"Could you spare something to eat? I haven't eaten in days," Zach said.

"We don' want no trouble, massa," the man said.

Three small heads peered out of the screen door, "You git back in there and stay," the woman said.

Zach did not advance farther. "I don't mean you any harm," he said. "I'm just hungry is all."

The couple looked at each other. The woman shook her head, hard, but the man seemed to soften. He was young and muscular and wore a pair of tattered bibbed dungarees, one strap missing. The woman was pretty, her skin lighter, dressed in a thin cotton frock that showed her figure in the light breeze.

"A little food and I'll be on my way," Zach said.

"Ellie, you go git a cup of milk, an' I'll pull some carrots an' maybe dig a tater," the man said.

The woman named Ellie glared at her husband, gathered her skirts, and stalked off toward the house. Her husband invited Zach to come and sit in the shade of the shed.

"You a soldier?" he asked.

"Well, I used to be."

"Confed'rate?"

"Yankee. I escaped from a prison several days ago."

The man looked relieved. "You excape from that pris'n over that way?" he asked, gesturing to the west.

"More of a hellhole than a prison."

"Ellie, com'n out here. Th' man's a Yankee," he said.

Ellie yelled out through the closed screen, "What difference does that make?"

"Oh, Ellie, can't you see? This man means us no harm," the man said.

The screen door slammed as the woman approached, still cautious, followed by three children, all clinging to her legs, obviously curious about the stranger. They were girls. Each one had her hair done up in different pigtails, tipped with ribbons. All three were dressed in brightly colored, ironed dresses. As the girls peeked at Zach from behind their mother's dress, Zach winked, and the girls hid, giggling.

When Zach saw the family, and how clean and neat they were, he realized how he must look to them. He quickly brushed the dried mud off his clothes and ran his hands through his hair.

"I'll pluck a chicken. Ellie, you fry it the way you always do, fix some grits, an' we'll fill this good man up."

The man went into the far shed and Ellie went back inside, leaving the three girls, who now hid behind a corner of the shed, continuing to steal peeks at the stranger. Each time they peeked, Zach winked, and they hid again. He beckoned them with his finger. The smallest of the three shyly came out of hiding, her two pigtails sticking up in the air, tiny pink ribbons bobbing.

"You are a very pretty young lady," Zach said. "You look like your mother. How old are you?"

The little girl bashfully held up four fingers, and the other two came out of hiding.

"And how old are you?" he asked the newcomers.

One held up five fingers and the oldest, six. "We got three cows," the five-year-old said, proudly holding up three fingers.

"An' a wadermel'n patch," the youngest added.

"Ar daddy's a free man," the oldest said.

Zach heard the clucking of a chicken as the man chased it inside the shed. Then "thwack" as an axe came down. "You girls ever heard the story about Jack and the Beanstalk?" he asked.

When they all three shook their heads no, he told the story. They kept moving closer to him, engrossed in the fairy tale. After Hansel and Gretel, one girl sat on each of his knees, and the other sat directly in front of him. He told the story of Little Red Riding Hood, and they cuddled up to him even closer when the big bad wolf appeared. Their hair tickled the bottom of Zach's chin. Time flew by and he told all the stories he could remember.

Zach could hear the sizzle of lard in the frying pan and the aroma of the frying chicken wafted through the air.

"Dinnah," Ellie yelled. "You girls wash up."

The father, who had been watching from the garden, approached. "Name's Joshua," he said holding out his hand.

"Zach, here." They shook and headed inside for dinner.

At the end of the meal, after the girls had wandered off, Zach said, "Ellie, that was the best meal I've had in years. Thank you. I know you took a risk just feeding me, so I'd best be going."

"Oh, please stay a while longer. And, here, take another piece, Massa Zach," Ellie said. "You haven't said a word 'bout the war. Tell us the news. We heard Genr'l Sherman is a goin' to attack Atlanta. Is that right?"

"Sorry, I know very little about the war. Being locked up and all, we didn't hear much. Sherman attacking Atlanta? That is big news. Do you know any more about it?"

"No," Joshua said. "Massa Zach, where you headed?"

"Abbeville, South Carolina. Ever heard of it?"

"Can't say as I ever have. You, Ellie?" said Joshua.

With a frown on her face, Ellie said, "Joshua Jefferson, why you sayin' you ne'er herd of Abbeville? You knows my grandpappy was from near Abbeville. How could you forget?"

Joshua looked embarrassed, his eyes begging her forgiveness.

She turned to Zach. "Yes, Massa Zach, we know 'bout Abbeville."

Zach reached into his pocket and pulled out the logbook, still wrapped in the canvas. As he did, mud from the river spilled onto the floor. "Oh, Massa Zach, your clothes need a washing. Why not stay in the shed tonight while I do that? You can be off in the morning," Ellie said.

"What have you there?" Joshua asked.

Zach opened the logbook. It was damp, but the tintype was dry. He was glad he had wrapped it so well in the canvas. He showed it to the couple, but neither could say they had ever seen her.

"Can you tell me how far it is to Abbeville?"

"I imagine it's a couple hundred miles that way," Ellie said pointing northeast.

"What about Atlanta?" Zach asked.

"Straight that way," she said pointing north. "Now you and Joshua go to the shed, and Joshua can give me your clothes. They should be dry by morning. Here, take this blanket."

Zach shrugged, "Sure is kind of you, Ellie."

In the shed, while Zach was getting undressed, he asked Joshua if any Confederates were in the area. Joshua replied that he saw them regularly, and they were always looking for deserters. He cautioned Zach that if they found him, they would hang him on the spot, whether he was a deserter or an escapee. Zach was certain Joshua was right. With Sherman invading the South, some Rebels would desert just to go home and protect their families. Others would be war weary soldiers who could already guess the outcome.

At dusk, Joshua spread some straw on the floor of the shed for Zach to sleep on. With the blanket wrapped around him, Zach thought about what he would do in the morning. The little shed had a separate pen inside that held a young calf Joshua was trying to wean. The calf was restless, moving around and around its pen, calling for its mother. Zach wondered if General Sherman would remember him.

17

Knoxville, Tennessee, 1908

CHRIS COULD HEAR the morning edition of "*The Sentinel*" being loaded onto wagons just below his window as he finished writing his next article. He had left the window open to let the cool air in to help him stay awake. It was four o'clock in the morning. The pot of coffee he had ordered was dry. He had written all night.

He leaned back in his chair and reread the section where Zach described Colonel Wirz. While Chris's assignment was to uncover the Zach Harkin mystery, his reporter's instincts told him the story was bigger than anybody back in New York thought. Zach had been in a unique position to learn things about Wirz that no other inmate knew. Wirz was the only man hanged for war crimes after the war, and Chris wondered if all the facts were generally known. Wirz had been powerless to feed and clothe the inmates. He had a human side. Was the North ready to believe it? Was his editorial board ready to print it?

Chris took out a fresh sheet of stationary:

Dearest Sarah,

Zach's story continues to unfold with interesting twists. I won't tell you the details so you can read all about it in the Sunday edition.

I don't know for sure when I will get back to New York, but it won't be more than another week or so. So anxious to see you and share our bed.

One more time, Miss Sarah Barnwell Elliott, I love you. How does Mrs. Sarah Elliott Martin sound to you?

Chris

He lay on his bed and tried to sleep. His hands were still shaky from all the coffee he'd drunk. He thought about Sarah. While he was from northwest Georgia, she was from the central part of the state. Milledgeville, the original capital. While he had lost most of his Southern drawl, Sarah had kept hers and was proud of it. Maybe that was why he loved her. Her fierce independence was unlike any other woman he ever knew. She cared very little about what people thought of her. She believed women should have equal rights, and supported the women's suffrage movement. She had worked with Susan B. Anthony, and tried to carry on her work in New York City after Anthony died in 1906.

They had known each other casually before, but when Chris was assigned to cover various Suffrage demonstrations in the city, their friendship blossomed. One night after having dinner together, she had spent the night with Chris at his apartment. Two days later, when he came home from work, she had moved in. She said only that she wanted to live with him and nothing more. He was delighted; however, he was certain Sarah's father, and especially her grandfather, never would have approved.

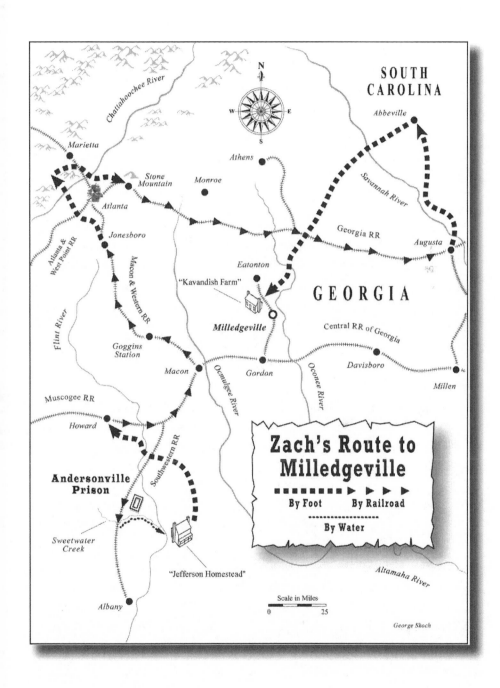

18

Near Atlanta, Georgia 1864

THE SLOW, LABORING engine chugged into the tiny train station in the little hamlet of Howard, Georgia. The train, loaded with war materiel for Johnston's Army of Tennessee and supplies for the besieged city of Atlanta, was making its first stop on the one hundred-six mile run from Macon to Atlanta. It was mid-morning in late August; moisture in the air hung like steam under the fruit-laden pecan trees surrounding the west side of the depot. The air was still and the smoke from the engine lay like a horizontal cloud a few feet above the ground. "Macon & Western" was painted in yellow below the engineer's window.

Already sweating, Zach sat under a tree, watching several soldiers board as the train took on water. He had left the Jefferson homestead several weeks before, wearing the clean clothes Ellie had washed. The simple act of donning clean dungarees and a shirt was a previously forgotten pleasure. They had given him some food in a gunnysack, which he consumed in the first three days. After that, he'd managed by stealing from vegetable gardens along the way, and by foraging for wild nuts and berries. He had rolled up one pant leg and tied the gunnysack around his knee. After he crafted a forked tree limb into a crutch, he looked like any other wounded soldier.

Zach limped onto the last train car and found a seat next to a young soldier who did not appear to be wounded. The soldier was dirty, sullen, and quiet. He did not acknowledge Zach. The train pulled out, heading toward Crawford, seven miles away. The man next to Zach stared impassively at the seat ahead of him.

The train was scheduled to stop in Smarr, but steamed through, stopping at the next station, Collins. More soldiers got on. There was much excited talk among them about Sherman trying to flank Hood to cut off supply lines to Atlanta. The stranger next to Zach did not move. Zach stole another glance, and noticed his chin was quivering and tears streaking his mud-caked face. Zach put his hand on the man's arm, "War ain't no fun, is it?" he said.

As if a wellspring had opened, the man buried his head in his hands and wept, his body tense and heaving. Zach put his hand on the man's back. "I'm here if you want to talk about it," he said softly.

The sobbing slowed. "Goddamned Yankees," he said, almost inaudibly.

"What happened? Where were you?"

"Chattanooga," he said. Zach waited for him to continue. "They got my father."

"Go on," Zach said.

"He was a first lieutenant. We had four cannon and were engaged just across Peachtree Creek. We wanted to catch them while they were crossing. We were all set up and commenced firing, making good use of our limited ammunition. Then we came under fire, and one of our spongers didn't get the barrel clean. The next load misfired, killing the sergeant. My dad rushed over to fill in and got shot. Right through the head. Never had a chance."

The train whistled for the next stop and the brakes started to squeal.

"Yankee infantry?" Zach asked.

"Chickenshit sharpshooter."

Zach felt as if he had been hit in the gut by a twenty-pound cannon ball. He pulled his hand back, turned the other way, and tried to breathe. The young man stared at him as the train screeched to an abrupt stop and somebody outside shouted, "Goggins Station!"

Both men sat in silence as the train chugged through Burnsville, Milner, Griffin, and Lovejoy Stations. The leg from Lovejoy Station to the next stop, Jonesborough, was six miles, and about half of it was through a dense pine forest.

Zach's head shot forward as the train's brakes squealed, coming to an unexpected stop. Two of the passengers in Zach's car stepped off to investigate and yelled back through the windows that the track had been blown up. Then dozens of Union cavalry stormed out of the woods from both sides, sabers drawn, surrounding the train. Without firing a shot, the officer in charge rode down the line and ordered everyone to disembark and form a line.

As Zach stepped down, he noticed an old woman getting off the car in front. She appeared to be the only female on the train and she was having trouble making the last step down. He went to assist and they stood together while the officer appeared to be trying to figure out what to do with the passengers as a whole and the old lady in particular. After some conversation with one of his sergeants, the lieutenant announced that all passengers were to walk in single file, following the lead rider, who lead them into the woods. He told the woman to get back on the train. Sometime later, they came to a clearing and the more severely wounded soldiers were separated out and left there.

Walking in a westerly direction, Zach hobbled with eight others through the thick trees for several hours until they were told to rest. The trees shaded the men from the blistering sun, but the air was humid and oppressive, Zach's clothing was wet from perspiration. One of the soldiers asked each man's name and unit identification. Zach replied he had been with the U.S.S.S.

"Are you saying you are a Union soldier?" The man asked.

"Yes."

"What does U.S.S.S. mean anyway?"

"I was a sharpshooter," Zach whispered.

"A sharpshooter? Why were you on that train?"

"I was a prisoner at Camp Sumter. Maybe you know it as Andersonville," Zach said.

The soldier pushed his hat back and scratched his head. His hair was wet, and he was obviously uncomfortable in the heat. He looked back at his sergeant, as if unsure how to proceed.

"You were a Rebel prisoner? Where and when were you captured?" The sergeant asked.

"In the hills of Tennessee, just northeast of Knoxville. Several months ago."

"Hey, Lieutenant, did you hear that? Were there any U.S.S.S. even in Tennessee 'several months ago'?"

The lieutenant joined them, "Who was your commander?" he asked.

"Colonel Hiram Berdan."

"Never heard of him." The lieutenant sounded doubtful.

Nobody said anything, then Zach said, "I know General Sherman."

The soldiers looked incredulous. If they had suspected Zach was lying before, now they were sure.

With the cavalrymen on horseback, the prisoners were marched through the rest of the day and into the night. The riders were initially cautious, but as they marched, they seemed to relax. Zach assumed they were back in Union-controlled territory. They were given a light ration and told they would resume their march in the morning.

Zach made a pile of pine needles to rest his head on. Some kind of record, he thought, being a prisoner of both sides of a war. At least he was on the Union side. If he could convince them he was not a Rebel, he just might be able to work his way east to Abbeville, wherever that was. The night air was cool and a soft breeze blew through the pines, lulling him to sleep.

He awoke to the musty smell of horses and leather. His body never got used to sleeping on the hard ground. His muscles ached and his skin prickled from lying on the needles. No rations were issued, but their march continued, headed north, the sun's rays shining through the moist air, showing the way. They arrived at a stream, and all the prisoners drank deeply, not knowing when they would get another chance.

By noon, they had reached a large camp, possibly for a whole regiment. There they were put into a roped-off pen with other prisoners and told they would be moving out later in the day.

A bit later, the lieutenant came by, accompanied by another lieutenant.

"Tell the lieutenant here what unit you were with," he said.

"Second United States Sharpshooters," Zach replied. "Under Colonel Hiram Berdan."

The second lieutenant said that he knew Berdan and asked Zach to describe him.

"Tall, slender, mustache, light blue eyes," Zach said.

"That could describe a lot of folks," the man said. "Anything else?"

"Yeah. He's an arrogant son-of-a-bitch."

The lieutenant stared at Zach for a moment and Zach thought he had made a mistake. Then he smiled, "By God, you do know him. Get him out of here."

They went to stand by a fire and a sergeant gave him some hot food. Chicken cooked in bacon fat. Zach ate hungrily, licking his fingers.

"Now what about this claim of yours that you know General Sherman?" the same lieutenant asked.

"Do you have a pencil and paper?" Zach asked.

The sergeant left and soon returned and handed Zach some.

Zach drew two concentric circles on the paper, then punched five small holes close to the center. On the bottom, he wrote: *1000 yards Zach Harkin (Shiloh)*.

"Give this to the general. I think he will remember me."

The sergeant took the paper and left.

Soon, a major approached Zach and said, "Harkin? It's been quite a while since Shiloh. What are you doing here?"

"Major McCoy. You look a bit better than the last time I saw you," Zach said.

"Yep. Recovered nicely since that Minie ball after Shiloh. You went east to the Sharpshooters. I don't see any uniform on you. You still in?"

General Sherman walked up to McCoy as if to tell him something, and when he saw Zach, he said. "Harkin. Heard you were in these parts. What the hell happened?" He was pointing at the new scar on Zach's face.

"Just a little misunderstanding, sir."

Sherman was hatless, his face tanned and weathered. He had the same grizzled, short red beard, but to Zach he appeared different. He spoke more distinctly and wasn't as nervous as he had been the last time they met. He seemed confident in his position.

Sherman did not offer his hand, so Zach saluted.

"Sir," Zach said with a smile.

SCARRED

"Never will forgive that damn brother of mine for shipping you east." The general headed toward his tent, motioning for Zach to come along. "You were captured? Escaped Andersonville?"

"Yes. Long story, sir."

"Talk about Andersonville. I hear it's a hellhole. And nobody escapes."

"Yes to the first; no to the second, Sir," Zach said with a slight smile. "And to say Andersonville is a hellhole makes it sound much better than it is, sir."

"Drop the goddamned 'Sir,' Harkin."

Zach remembered that Sherman had used the exact same line two years before, when they met at Shiloh. "Some things never change, Sir. I mean, General," Zach said, still smiling.

Sherman sat down at a table set with his noonday meal. "Sit down, son," he said. "Have you eaten?"

Zach sat down and indicated that he had.

"How many prisoners?" The general asked.

"Probably upward of twenty-five thousand. Every morning, they'd carry out five or six hundred dead, maybe more. Some days, there were no food rations. No good water, and the latrine is a little stream that barely flows. The stench is overwhelming."

"What about this guy, Wirz? I hear he is some kind of real bastard."

"He may not be as bad as they say, Sir. I mean—"

They talked on for several minutes about the number of guards and the surrounding landscape. Sherman made some notes.

"How did you like Berdan?" Sherman asked, shifting the subject.

"Mind if I don't answer that?" Zach said.

"How did you get caught, son?" Sherman asked.

"I was mustered out after Gettysburg, Sir. Lost my nerve." It felt like a confession. Zach stared at his feet.

"Go on," Sherman said.

Zach searched for words. "Guess I'm too much of a weakling, Sir," he said, his eyes watering.

Sherman had finished eating. He paused, then got up and put his hand on Zach's back and said in a fatherly tone, "Sick of killing, ain't you? This goddamned war. I'm doing everything I can to end it. The sooner it's over, the sooner the healing can start."

Zach pulled out the logbook and opened it to the picture of the woman. "This is the wife of one of the last men I shot, Sir. I would like to find her and her family."

With a bit of impatience, Sherman said, "You don't have to feel that way, Harkin. Hell, if all my men felt that way, I wouldn't have an army." He studied Zach's face for a moment and said, "But you do what you have to. I will give you safe passage to move around." He turned to McCoy and was already off on another subject.

While Zach waited for the safe passage, he asked Major McCoy where Abbeville, South Carolina was located. To Zach's surprise, McCoy knew exactly where it was. He unrolled a map on top of a table. The map was long and narrow. On the westernmost part of the map was Atlanta and the easternmost was Savannah. McCoy traced his finger east to Athens, then just over the South Carolina line.

"Right here's Abbeville. Why do you ask?"

"I'm going there," Zach said.

"You can't go there, it's beyond our lines. You'd be in enemy territory."

"Major, I've been in enemy territory for the last four months. I can manage. If you were going there, how would you go?"

"You're a stubborn cuss," he said. "If it were me, I would go north around Atlanta, like this, then head south to the first railroad. That'll be the Georgia Railroad, and you can pick it up here at Stone Mountain. Take the train to Augusta, then head north to Abbeville, right here," he said, outlining the route with his finger.

Zach studied the map. *Not far*, he thought. He could be there in a week— unless something went wrong.

19

Near Atlanta, Georgia

SKIRTING TO THE north of besieged Atlanta, Zach could see Stone Mountain clearly, just east of the city. Stone Mountain was a giant, granite dome. It looked like a mushroom popping out of the surrounding soil. On top was a tower that surveyed the entire area. Zach had assumed the character of a wounded soldier again, with a wrapped knee and a crutch. The train station was crowded with civilians fleeing Atlanta for the comparative safety of Athens and Augusta.

"Excuse me," he said to an old man in line to purchase a ticket. "Is this line for the train to Augusta?"

"Yes," he said. "But no tickets are available. I am trying to get a ticket for the train after that."

"Why the rush?"

"General Hood is leaving us. He's retreating and giving the whole city to Sherman so he can burn it."

When the train arrived, it was already full, with passengers standing in the cars and even some standing on the steps. People surged to get on, trying to force their way in. Zach hobbled to the front of the train and looked in at the engineer. "Any room in the coal car?" he yelled.

The engineer came down to the last step. "Hurry," he whispered. "Let me help you. Don't want anymore passengers, but I always try to accommodate the wounded."

Thankful to be on the train at all, Zach crawled up on top of the wood-pile. He thought about the irony of wood in a coal car, and the shortage of basic materials caused by the ugly war. The smoke from the boiler passed overhead, but the ash fell on Zach whenever the train slowed.

The setting sun reflected off the high brick chimney of the Confederate Powder Works as Zach got off the train in Augusta. The engineer had told him the factory produced most of the gunpowder used by the Confederacy, and proudly stated that it was almost the largest such factory in the world. With little breeze, the dark, heavy, smoke fell to the ground, as if to reinforce the sense of despondency the Southern population felt.

Zach crossed the Savannah River into South Carolina and headed north along a road he was told led to Abbeville, arriving midday two days later. It was Sunday, and the square at the heart of town was strangely still, all businesses being closed for the Sabbath. The livery was the only exception.

The proprietress, a middle-aged woman, was pitching manure into a wagon hooked up to a mule. The mule looked as if it had not been fed for some time, each of its ribs was clearly visible. She stopped when she saw Zach limping toward her. "You oughta be in church," she said, leaning heavily on her pitchfork. She smiled, "You look like you could use some religion." Her faded cotton dress was formless and covered with brown smudges, her greying hair was wet with perspiration.

"You're probably right, ma'am, but I wonder if you can help me."

"Don't have any horses," she said. "All of them been confiscated. Even my mule team. All I got left is ole' Jeff here, and he's on his last legs. Don't have much oats either. All gone for the damned war," she said.

Zach pulled out the logbook, opened it, and showed her the photograph. "I'm looking for this lady. I was told she might be from this area."

"Name's Maud, by the way," she said, taking the book from Zach. "Hmmm—pretty young thing, isn't she? Why you so interested?"

Zach hesitated. "Guess you could say I knew her husband."

"Knew him? Sounds like he's a goner. So many men—" She didn't lift her eyes from the picture. With a frown, she said, "Can't say that I know her. You say she's from these parts?"

"The only thing I know for certain, ma'am, is that her husband was in McGowan's Brigade."

"Sam McGowan's Brigade? Now we're gettin' somewhere. Yep, Sam and Susie live just down the street. You can almost see their house from here. Sam was here just last year recovering from a bad wound. Shot in the leg. They almost had to take it off, but they didn't. He's up in Virginia somewhere."

"You think Mrs. McGowan would know her?"

"She just might. She's probably home from church by now. Go ask her. It's the second house on the right."

———

The door was opened by a little girl wearing a full-length flowered dress. I'm looking for Susan McGowan," Zach said with a slight bow.

"I'm Susan McGowan," the little girl said. "But I suppose you're looking for my mom."

Her mother appeared from the other room. She wore an identical dress to the little girl's and was holding her bonnet in her hand. "Yes, can I help you?" she said, looking up at Zach's scarred face and glancing down at his leg. "Come on in out of the sun."

The smell of frying bacon mixed with the lilac flagrance she was wearing. Zach thought of his mother, who had always liked the smell of lilacs. "I'm trying to find this lady." He handed the picture to her. "I'm told her husband was in your husband's brigade."

"Why, this is Martha Kavandish, from Milledgeville. Her husband, Jack, was one of my husband's best sharpshooters. Did you know him?"

"Er—yes, you could say I knew him."

"He was killed, you know. Up in Virginia somewhere, just before Chancellorsville. Shot by another sharpshooter, we hear. Poor Martha. She was devastated. What with the young boy and all. Now she has that farm to run. Haven't seen her in a while. What a nice girl she is."

"You seem to know her well," Zach said.

"I try to know all of Sam's boys," she said. "But Jack and Martha were easy to remember. Such a happy couple—"

"I found his logbook. It had her picture in it. I would like her to have it," he said, handing it to her.

"Oh, aren't you sweet," she said, flipping through the pages. "Yes, I'm sure she would appreciate having it. You come a long way to get here?"

"I'm from Tennessee, ma'am. Eastern Tennessee."

"Oh dear. Way over there in Tennessee. My goodness," she said. Then she looked toward the kitchen. "Well Mister aah—what did you say your name was?"

"Zach, Zach Harkin."

"Heavens to Betsy, Zach Harkin, you just sit down there," she said pointing to a settee. "You are staying for breakfast. We always have breakfast right after Sunday services. We are so hungry for news. Susie, we have a guest. Please set another place, honey."

Zach didn't want to stay. He was afraid of all the questions. But how could he refuse? He sat down. "Thank you ma'am," he said. "Sure smells good."

Susie came in and shyly crawled up to sit next to him. She wore black patent leather shoes with buckles. As she sat back, her feet barely hung over the edge of the settee. "Mommy says we're going to lose the war. Do you think those Yankees will kill us all?"

"Those Yankees would never harm a cute little girl like you," Zach said.

She ducked her head, then looked up at Zach. "Where did you get that scar, Mister Zach?"

"Over in Georgia."

She reached up and touched it with her finger. "Does it hurt?"

"It used to."

She moved her finger and felt his beard. "You could use a shave, Mister Zach."

Zach smiled. He interlocked his hands together with his two index fingers pointing up, "Here's the church, here's the steeple, open it up, and see all the people," he said.

Susie squealed with delight. "Tell me another, Mister Zach."

Mrs. McGowan peeked through the door, "Breakfast is served. Susie, escort our guest to the table like a young lady."

Susie escorted him to the head of the table. "You can sit here," she said. "This is Daddy's seat."

To the delight of Mrs. McGowan, Zach ate everything put in front of him. She wanted to know about the war, and Zach told her what he knew about Chattanooga, the siege and possible fall of Atlanta, and Hood replacing Johnston. When she asked how and where he was wounded, Zach skirted the questions, saying it was an ugly war and he preferred not to talk about it in front of two beautiful ladies.

Zach learned that Martha Kavandish's son was five years old, that she and her husband had been married for only a year before he went to war. They had a thirty-acre farm, but with all the men gone to war, it was hard for Martha to manage it on her own. They had a slave her parents had given them as a wedding gift. He was a hard worker but slight and frail, so it took both of them to do the heavy work. Mrs. McGowan also explained that Jack had been a very hard worker and provided well for his family. He loved to shoot and hunt game and he had looked forward to taking his son out as soon as he was old enough.

Zach thanked Mrs. McGowan for her hospitality, gave Susie a warm hug and, armed with directions to the Kavandish farm, left in the midafternoon. She had told him it might take a few days to get there, and had given him some things to eat along the way. After crossing back over the Savannah River into Georgia, Zach headed southwest. The farm was north of Milledgeville, on the Oconee River, about one hundred miles away.

20

Knoxville, Tennessee, 1908

The Lamar Hotel lobby was crowded when Chris returned. He looked toward the bar. It was packed with people celebrating. Jerome was behind the reception counter.

"What's the occasion?" Chris asked.

"We got Governor Patterson staying here tonight. There's a reception in there, and the booze is free. Even our own mayor is here. He's a good guy. Served with him at Shiloh."

"Free booze?"

"Yeah, but you gotta be from Tennessee," Jerome said with a smile. "By the way, here's a telegram for you. Just came in."

Chris quickly glanced at the telegram. It was terse:

Mr. Martin,

Cannot print your report on Col Wirz. Are you trying to revise history? Rewrite it.

J. Pulitzer

Jerome headed toward the bar, still smiling and said, "This is one time I'll buy. You coming?"

Chris, trying to think of his response to Pulitzer, declined and went to his room. He sat on the bed, and reread the telegram. He'd met Joseph Pulitzer only one time, but he knew he ruled the newspaper with an iron fist. His signature meant that the last installment had reached the highest scrutiny. He sat down at the table, and cleaned his dark-rimmed glasses while he pondered what he was going to do.

He picked up his pen and started to write, but got up abruptly and went back to the Harkin gun shop.

A middle-aged man answered Chris's knock. Tall and lanky, he was clean-shaven, with neatly combed, dark brown hair. "Mister Martin?" The man said.

"Is Zach here?" Chris asked.

"He took a walk. Be back soon. Come in. I'm Tom."

They shook. Chris looked back toward the door, "Are you the son of 'Zach Harkin & Son" on the door?"

"That's me," Tom said, motioning for Chris to sit. "Dad and I started another place in Nashville, and I spend most of my time there. He told me about you."

"He has quite a story to tell. My paper is printing several hundred thousand extra copies every time an edition has more of his story."

Tom took a step toward Chris for emphasis. "All of this is opening up a lot of old wounds, Mr. Martin."

Chris hesitated.

"Do you think all this digging up the past will do Dad any good? Or is this all about you?"

"Well, a lot of people want to know what happened to your dad back in sixty-four," Chris said.

"All I care about is my dad," Tom said.

The room was silent. The ticking of the clock in the next room was the only sound.

Chris didn't know what to say.

Finally, the sound of Zach's footsteps, and the rear screen door slammed shut.

Seeing the two men together, Zach said, "I see you two have met."

Happy for the interruption, Chris said, "Yep, just getting acquainted."

The three men sat in awkward silence.

Eventually, Tom said he had some work to do and went into another room.

"What brings you back this evening, Chris?" Zach said.

Chris explained that his editors were questioning the experience with Colonel Wirz, and he wanted to make sure his notes were correct. They reviewed the conversation between the two soldiers and Wirz the day they came into Wirz's office out of the rain. Zach confirmed Chris had it exactly right.

Back at the Lamar front desk, Chris wrote a short telegram to his editor: "The story stands. C.M."

Up in his room, Chris changed into his nightclothes and got into bed. He lay there, his mind whirling, mulling over the day's events. He wondered if he would have a job in the morning.

21

Near Milledgeville, Georgia, 1864

THE FARMHOUSE WAS nestled in a copse of cottonwoods midway between the road and the river. The river shimmered in the sunlight, flowing south. A light breeze rattled the leaves and smoke rose from the chimney into the cool, September morning air. The space between the two dusty wheel tracks that led to the barn had grown over with weeds. The barn was sturdy, but the paint was faded. Zach saw a semicircle scraped in the dirt in front of the barn and deduced the door hinge was loose. Standing just outside the large barn doors, he saw a black man driving out the cotter pin of a broken wagon wheel. His face and arms glistening with sweat. The wheel was nearly as big as he was. Some of the shingles on an adjacent shed were loose, breaking the neat, parallel lines of the roof. A garden next to the shed contained tomatoes, beans, and squash, all plump and ready for the table.

Two monarch butterflies hovered over bee balm flowers in a pot hanging from the front porch eave as Zach approached the house. Zach's chest heaved with anticipation as he stepped up on the small porch.

A young woman opened the wooden door wide, but remained standing inside the screen door, her brown eyes quickly appraising the stranger in front of her. Her long brunette hair was swept back off her face with two silver barrettes just behind her ears. She wore a gingham dress, full on the bottom, covered by an apron tied at the waist. The bodice of her dress swept just low enough to hint at a lovely figure. Her rounded brows yielded to a high forehead, two tiny curls tickling her cheekbones, leading to her perfectly-rounded jaw and chin, and framing her pert nose. Her face was flushed from working in the kitchen. When she saw Zach, her hands went to her hair as if searching for something out of place.

After a slight pause, she said, "Yes?" Her voice was soft but firm. Her accent heavy.

"I was at Chancellorsville," Zach said.

"Oh. Oh, my. Why, please come in," she said, pushing the screen door open and inviting Zach into her parlor, where she motioned him to sit. As he sat, he looked self-consciously at his shoes, covered in red dust, and his britches, which hadn't been washed in weeks. She sat on a small bench nearby facing him, and put her hands together and rested them on her knees. She waited for him to speak, knowing it was about her dead husband, Jack.

Zach ran his fingers over the upholstery tacks in the chair's arms, searching for the right words. The small parlor looked infrequently used. A full sized grandfather clock ticked in the corner. The broad-planked floor was covered with rag rugs. On one end of the room was a roll-top desk. A framed picture of Jack in full uniform sat atop it. Jack with his rifle, a beautiful, scoped Whitworth. Zach had never seen him before he shot him, and the image of the man's living face startled him.

Zack took the logbook from his pocket and handed it to her without saying a word. She opened it slowly. Her picture fell to the floor, and as she read the first few entries, tears welled and flowed down her cheeks. She flipped to the last entry, which read: March 3: ...*Two more days and I'm on two week leave. Seems like an eternity since I've seen her...* She closed the book, put her hands over her face, and wept.

"Mommy? W-w-what's wrong?" A little boy ran into the room and to his mother's side. She put her arm around him, held him tight, and continued to sob. The boy looked over at Zach as if angry he had caused his mother to cry.

Composing herself, Martha said, "Tommy, this man knew your father. He brought us his diary. Introduce yourself."

The little boy strode directly over to Zach, stuck out his hand, and said, "I-I-I'm Tom Kavandish. Were you in the w-w-war with my d-d-dad?"

Zach shook his hand and told him his name then reached over and mussed up his black hair. "You must be the man of the house," he said. The boy went back to his mother, put his arm around her, looked back at Zach, and nodded.

"I don't recall Jack ever mentioning your name, Mister Harkin. Were you in his unit?" she asked.

"Not exactly, ma'am, but I was the first to see him after he was… I cannot tell you how sorry I am." Having no idea what to say or do next, Zach stood and said, "I'd best be going, ma'am."

"Please, call me Martha," she said. "How on earth did you find us?"

"Wasn't easy," he said, and he told her about the crowded trains out of Atlanta and his visit with Susan McGowan and how she had given him directions to the farm. He told her the news about Hood vacating the city, and the expectation that Sherman would burn the entire area. She watched him closely, absorbing every word. He found himself repeating some of the things he had already told her, but in more detail.

Zach had sat back down when the hissing sound of a pot boiling over came from the kitchen. "Oh, my. The stew!" Martha ran into the kitchen, leaving Tommy and Zach alone.

Zach looked around the room. "Looks like you're doing a good job seeing after things, Tommy," he said.

"M-my daddy h-had to go t-to the war," he said. His matter of fact expression showed no sadness, but rather a sense of pride. He had his mother's large brown eyes and her skin, but his father's black hair. He seemed frustrated when he could not pronounce words clearly, so he tried to force them, compounding the problem.

On a table beside his chair was a toy wagon and a building block set. The wagon was mounted on four wheels and had a pull string. Zach took the wagon and sat on the floor, "Bet you can build a barn like yours."

Tommie squatted down in front of Zach and started to build. He laid the foundation, and left an open section for the large door, but was puzzled as to how to construct the hip roof. Zach pointed at a piece that might help and the boy quickly grabbed it and continued.

Martha came in from the kitchen and hesitated, seeing the two on the floor, "Mister Harkin, you've come all this way, would you have some stew with us before you go?"

The kitchen was the biggest room in the house. Just inside the backdoor was a bench with jackets and hats hanging above it. Boots covered with red dust were lined up under the bench. One large pair sat alone. A square, cast iron stove sat against the outside wall with a kettle on top. A nearly empty wood box sat next to a copper boiler full of water. The smell of the rich stew mixed with wood smoke made Zach realize how hungry he was. A table in the middle of the kitchen had three chairs around it and three place settings. Martha indicated to Zach to sit in the middle and she ladled stew into each bowl.

Martha talked about the farm.

Heavy spring rains had caused the river to flood, covering the fields between the river and the farmhouse. Rains continued, and the river did not recede for ten days, ruining her corn crop. The peanut crop in front of the house, however, had thrived, and was near harvest. Her team of horses had been confiscated by the government, and all she had left was her mule, Jake. Most slaves in her area had been impressed into service, but, her slave, Levon, was considered too small, and they let her keep him.

"Levon and Jake are all I have to run this place," Martha said. "And of course, Tommy. Tommy is a big help." She smiled at her son. "He keeps the wood box full, the stove fire goin', and all sorts of things. Don't you, Tommy?"

"I saw Levon on the way in. Looks like a hard worker," Zach said.

"Gracious, me. I've been talking about me all this time. What about you, Mister Harkin?"

Zach avoided the question, and instead talked about the probable fall of Atlanta and the subsequent fall of the Confederacy. Tommie got up to put a piece of wood in the stove. The fire crackled, sending a hollow noise up the flue. The sun sank below the level of the cottonwoods and shone through the back door onto the wood-planked floor. The screen door had a typical wad of cotton attached at the center. Zach had always wondered why.

"Mister Harkin, I can see you don't like to talk about yourself much. Could I show you around our place?"

Zach ducked through the back door as they went outside into the cool evening. They walked toward the river, their feet sinking into the rich, loamy bottomland in the rear of the farm. The field toward the river, where Martha's corn crop had stood, was fallow and weedy. The field on the other side of the farmhouse was higher, and had a healthy crop of corn with large, succulent ears nearly ready for harvest. Zach had little actual experience farming, but he knew a farmer's work was difficult, and carried many risks.

They walked a loop through the backfield and headed toward the barn. Martha explained the various operations of the farm, and Zach realized her knowledge was limited. She had an optimistic outlook, but seemed not to grasp that she needed a lot more help than just Levon. With the 1864 Confederate call for any able-bodied male to conscript into the army, even old men weren't available to help with the hard work. Of course, most able-bodied slaves had been impressed by the government, so Martha could not even pay a neighbor for a borrowed slave's labor. Her farm had almost no chance of providing for the two of them, and Zach felt that burden resting squarely on his shoulders.

As dusk approached, they entered the barn where Levon was trying to remount the repaired wheel to the farm wagon. He had propped up the axle, but he hadn't the strength to lift the wheel into position, and just as he tried, the wagon slipped off the prop and fell. Levon had to release the wheel to avoid being crushed, and it rolled across the floor and came to rest on a pile of hay that Jake had been munching on. Jake brayed as if denied his dinner, adding to the confusion. To an outsider, the scene would have been comical, but to Zach, it was pathetic. Martha, Levon, and Jake trying to run the farm.

Zach picked up the wheel and leaned it against the wagon. He lifted the wagon axle, set it on his bended knee, and reached for the wheel. In one motion, the wheel was back on the wagon. Zach then asked Levon to reinsert the cotter pin, which he did with three taps of a mallet.

"Why, don't that beat all!" Martha said. "Just like that, you fixed it." Her brown eyes were wide with surprise.

Zach ran his hand over the cotter pin to be sure it was tight and pointed to the haystack in the corner, "Would you mind if I stay the night? I can sleep right over there."

She thought a moment, "Why sure, I guess so. Yes, that would be fine. You'll need a blanket, Mister Harkin."

22

Near Milledgeville, Georgia, 1864

I N THE EARLY morning light, all Zach could see was a large, round, wet object with two holes moving up and down only inches in front of his face. Each time the object moved up, he felt slimy sandpaper sliding over his face. He swiped at it and his hand hit something unyielding. Trying to sit up, he saw the large object was a cow. Levon stood next to the cow, laughing and slapping his leg in glee. Zach sat up, laughing, too, straw sticking in his hair and covering his clothes, his face still covered with cow saliva. A rooster crowed from one of the sheds, its rude announcement echoing off the trees by the river.

Before he had gone to sleep, Zach had learned that Levon was mute, which further explained why he had not been impressed and taken away by the Confederates. He had been given to Martha when they were both ten years old, and they had been inseparable, until at age of thirteen, when two white boys saw them together. Barely surviving the beating, Levon lost his voice and never grew again.

The fusty smell of old straw, mixed with the scents of dry earth and manure, reminded Zach of his boyhood. Low light filtering into the barn through the vertical boards showed each imperfection. Levon grabbed a three-legged stool and proceeded to milk the cow, his little fingers expertly stripping two teats at a time, milk ringing against the bottom of the pail. Even though Levon was probably in his early twenties, he looked and acted like a young boy.

Next to the attached corncrib was a small worktable with various tools mounted on wooden pegs on the wall behind it. Zach picked up the mallet

Levon had used the night before. He imagined the original owner using it, his hand on the handle, doing whatever job he had set out to do. No longer. He knew the dead man would visit him again that night.

Zach decided the first thing he would do was fix the barn door that had a loose hinge. He found a ladder between two barn beams, climbed up to the broken hinge, and pried it off. Then relocated it, using a hammer and six nails to secure the door tightly. He bent the protruding nails down against the wood on the back of the door.

Martha arrived, and when she realized that Zach was trying to help, she said, "I can't pay you." She wore the same gingham dress as the day before, but it looked fresh. Her face was again flushed from work, and he guessed she had been up for quite some time. As he came down the ladder, her hands went to her hair again.

"No need, ma'am, just doing a couple odd jobs. Not expecting anything in return."

"I have some porridge on the stove. Please come in. It isn't much, but it will stick to your ribs." She seemed uneasy.

At the house, Zach opened the screen door for her, and she gave him an expression that said, *I can open my own doors, thank you.* Zach sat in the same chair as the day before and Martha filled two bowls. She set one in front of Zach and took the other to the back door, where Levon was waiting. As Zach ate, Martha busied herself in the kitchen.

Zach saw her pause, looking out the window as if trying to find words, "Mister Harkin, I must ask, why are you here? Forgive me for being puzzled, but with the war going on, I would think you would be expected to support our boys out there, fighting this godforsaken war. To be truthful, I do not understand."

He took another spoonful into his mouth to buy some time. He stared straight ahead, "Ma'am, I am not a deserter if that is what you are worried about. Although I am sick of this war, I have never shirked my duty and obligation to my country. I would never do that. When I saw your dead husband, I was haunted by this war and what it does to the families of the gallant, dead soldiers. I saw your husband's logbook and read his last entry. When my commanding officer saw how I was affected, he gave me some time to try to find you."

"Must have been a very understanding commander."

"Yes," he said.

After a moment, she said, "Well, I guess we do have some good officers, and I am pleased he was so understanding. How much time do you have?"

"Couple of weeks, maybe. Time to get you set up for winter. Then I'd best go back."

She went to where Zach sat, the happy lilt in her voice returning, "Well, Mister Harkin, I am pleased." She put her hand on his arm. He felt the warmth of her touch, the warmth of her presence. He wanted a bath.

Tommy came into the kitchen, "Is Mister Harkin going to stay?" he asked.

"For a little while, Tommy," Zach said. The chair scraped on the floor as he stood. "I'd best get started, ma'am. Time's wasting," he said. "Thanks for breakfast. Please call me Zach." He felt her eyes on him as he walked out. He paused on the porch and took a deep breath. The warmth of the morning sun felt good.

Levon was slopping three hogs that Zach had not previously seen, their heads in a row, dipping in their trough, making contented sounds. Their bodies were covered in mud from a wallow just next to the trough. As each dipped its nose toward the slops, the others would push over to it, as if the food was better there. If one pushed too hard, the other would issue a high-pitched squeal in protest.

Zach motioned to Levon to come into the barn. He pointed to the mule just outside, and then to the plow in the corner, "Let's hitch him up," Zach said.

Levon gave a wide smile, grunted his understanding, and grabbed Jake's halter. Zach examined the plow while Levon attached the harness. On the beam was printed "Oliver Plow Works, South Bend, Indiana." He wondered how Jack had acquired it. The plow was a relatively new, single chisel foreshare, with a curved mainshare. Zach estimated that it could plow a swath of almost a foot. The handle was almost three feet wide and stood four feet high. Much too big for Levon to manage.

As they hitched the plow to the mule, Tommy appeared. "Are you going to plow? My daddy used to plow. Can I help?"

"Sure can, Tommy. Let's go. You'll be a big help."

They walked to the backfield, near the river. "Where did Jake get his name?" Zach asked Tommy.

Tommy broke into a grin, "Mom named him. She called him *Jake* because it sounded like *Jack*, my dad. Mom thought they both had the same amount of stubbornness."

Zach was worried that if the weeds were not plowed under before they went to seed, they would grow faster than the planted crop, come spring. He maneuvered Jake to the centerline of the field and told Tommy to run to the far side near the river and stand, so Jake would head straight toward him. When Tommy was in position, Zach guided Jake directly toward him, with the plowshare lowered into the soil. The rich, red loam flowed easily over the mainshare, forming a uniform furrow. It took Jake about five minutes to reach Tommy, and when Zach turned the corner to go back, the furrow was straight and true. Tommy followed on the return, and when they completed the first round, he asked Tommy if the river had any fish. Tommy said his dad had caught lots of big ones, so Zach instructed him to get a can and follow the plow to pick up worms. They would catch some fish for dinner, he said.

"Remember, big worms catch big fish," Zach said.

Zach worked the field through the morning. The higher the sun rose in the sky, the hotter it became. Around mid-morning, Zach pulled up and let Jake rest. He went to the river and drank, splashed his face with the cool water, and sat down against a tree. He felt better than he had in a long time. The physical exertion, working the soil, helping the family, all gave him a sense of exhilaration that he had not felt in years.

Tommy came out of the trees, "I know where they are," he said. "They're around that bend. Just past that big cottonwood. There's a hole there and the big ones are in there."

"You have a pole?"

"Dad had one. Guess it's mine now," said Tommy.

Zach got up and walked at a right angle to his last furrow, counting the steps. When he had counted fifty, he stopped and put a stick in the ground, then he told Tommy, when he had plowed to the stick, old Jake would be tired, so they could go fishing.

"Maybe your mommy could cook up a batch for supper," Zach said. "You be sure it's okay with her, and we'll have some fun."

Tommy's face lit up with excitement. He tore off to the house to tell his mother. Meanwhile, Zach and Jake continued to till the earth, rolling the weeds under with each round, and with each round, getting one foot closer to the stick. Once Jake got used to the routine, he would automatically turn at the end of a row, at which time Zach would lift the plow, then walk over to the return row and start back again. Around noon, Levon came out with some fried chicken and cool tea, and Zach ate hungrily. As he gave his empty glass back to Levon, he glanced back up to the house. He could see Martha in the doorway, watching.

The closer they got to the stick, the slower Jake went, and Zach had to push harder on the plow. When they finally got there, both needed to call it a day. While Zach put the mule out and wiped the harness off, Tommy waited near the barn door with the fishing pole and can of worms.

"Is it okay with your mother?" Zach asked.

"She said she's planning on having fish for supper, and if we don't catch any, we'll starve," Tommy said with a smile.

"Let's go," Zach said.

As Zach headed toward the river, Tommy ran ahead, then back, then around in circles. When they got to Tommy's fishing hole, Zach unwound the line off the pole, and as the line had no bobber, he tied a small stick above the hook. He looped a worm from Tommy's can onto the hook and told Tommy to throw it to the best spot.

The hole was located on a bend in the river and the water ran faster on the opposite side, making a large eddy in the hole, so the stick floated around in circles. Zach told Tommy to wait until the stick went under, then grab the pole, and pull up to set the hook. Tommy waited for the stick to disappear, his hands at the ready on both sides of the pole.

The stick continued to glide in broad circles.

After about ten minutes, Tommy's enthusiasm diminished and frustration hardened his features. Zach pulled up the line and set the stick higher, so the bait would hang lower in the water. Zach asked Tommy if his dad had taken him fishing, and Tommy said he'd been too young when he left. He barely remembered his father.

"Well, Tommy, your father was one of the best shots in the whole Rebel army. He could shoot the eyes out of a squirrel from two hundred yards."

Tommy was quiet.

A muskrat slid down the bank on the other side and swam down current, its tail like a snake behind it, only its nose and eyes above the water. Finally, nearing the bank, it disappeared into its den.

Zach and Tommy sat side-by-side. Tommy's feet fidgeted. Zach could feel the cool earth through his britches, his muscles relaxing from the long day of plowing. He remembered camping and fishing with his father back in eastern Tennessee. Tommy would never experience that.

Tommy was looking off the other way when the stick slowly came to a stop. It did not bob. "Tommy, look at the stick," Zach said.

"I d-don't s-see anything," Tommy said.

"It stopped. I think you might have a big fish eating the worm. He's so big he's in no hurry."

"W-w-what should I do?"

"Pick up the pole and lower the end toward the water so he can't feel the line." Tommy did as instructed.

"Now, don't jerk sideways, but pull up, to set the hook."

Zach watched the line go taut, and the pole dipped sharply in Tommy's grip. The fish dove deep and swam toward the other bank. Both Zach and Tommy were on their feet as the fish tugged hard, the pole dipping lower.

"Hold on tight," Zach yelled.

Tommy had no choice but to step forward, the pull was so strong, and as he did, his feet slipped out from under him and he fell into the water. He flailed on the surface and disappeared. Zach expected him to resurface, but only bubbles rose to the top and the surface flattened out as if the river had swallowed Tommy in one hungry gulp. Zach dove into the water near the spot where Tommy had gone under. The water was murky, but he flung his arms about, trying to cover as much space as possible. The water tasted like the river back in Tennessee: mud mixed with bitter leaves. He pushed off the bottom, and as he rose, he found Tommy and wrapped his arms around him. The boy's legs kicked, though his hands were out in front of him, rigid. They broke the surface, Zach gasping for air, and Tommy coughing and spitting. Zach grabbed him by the collar and pulled him to shallower water. When his feet gained traction, he hauled Tommy ashore and saw that he had not let go of the pole. The fish continued to pull, now heading back the opposite way into the deep water again.

Tommy was still coughing as Zach lifted him up on the bank. Tommy held the pole and the fish held its position as if in a stalemate.

"Okay, Tommy, slowly walk backwards, and when he comes close to the bank, I'll grab him."

Zach slipped back into the water as Tommy moved backward. When the fish was in reach, Zach grabbed it with both hands and threw it up on the bank. Tommy fell backwards, but quickly got up to survey his prize. The fish was a flat-head catfish. Zach estimated it weighed at least ten pounds. Tommy gaped wide-eyed and slack-jawed, water dripping off his face and clothes. The fish flopped on the damp ground, dirt sticking to its skin.

"C-can we eat him?" Tommy asked.

"You bet. Great job with this monster," Zach said. He reached for Tommy's pole, but Tommy's little fingers would not release it. Zach had to pry each little finger lose.

Tommy insisted on bringing the fish back to the house. He dragged it through the plowed field, refusing any help from Zach. When Tommy yelled to his mother to come out and see his fish, it looked like a large clod of dirt. Only its mouth, still gasping, gave any hint what it was. Tommy's brown eyes were wide, his chest expanded with pride.

"Why, gracious me! What have you boys gone and done?"

Zach smiled. "This old catfish went up against the best fisherman in these parts. Tommy caught it all by himself." He looked at Tommy's wet clothes, then his own. "Guess you could say it was an even fight," he said. "And the fish almost won."

"C-can we eat it? Tonight?" Tommy said.

Zach remembered that special feeling he had had as a boy when he brought home a squirrel or rabbit or other game and it was served for supper. Nothing ever tasted better.

23

Knoxville, Tennessee, 1908

ON THE WAY out the next morning, Chris confirmed that no telegrams had been sent to him in the night. A hotel umbrella kept his clothes dry on his short walk to the gun shop, but his shoes made squishing sounds as he entered and stood in front of the stove. He wiped his glasses with his handkerchief as Zach sat down beside him.

"Why do you think Sherman, a major general with what? Sixty? Eighty? A hundred thousand men under his command, would pay any attention to you?" Chris asked. "Back at Shiloh, you were a mere private. Why would he even give you the time of day?"

"Don't think I have never asked that question myself," Zach said. "I often wonder. Especially in Atlanta. At our first meeting at Shiloh, Sherman had no idea that he was going to be attacked and routed the next morning, but at Atlanta, he was in the middle of a complex duel with Johnston, and he had to feel the pressure. When I gave him his own telegram with my bullet holes in it from one thousand yards, I always remember the sly smile he got on his face.

"For some reason, he remembered and gave me some time with him and seemed to understand my motivation to find Jack's family. He was the hero of the West. His men adored him, knew he cared for them, and thought he could outsmart any Confederate general they put against him. But underneath all that, I think he was a real humanitarian. He thought the war would have to end before reconstruction could begin, and the sooner the war ended, the better."

"But his men raped and pillaged. How could you call that humanitarian?" Chris asked.

"Sherman wrote his memoirs in 1875, and one of the most interesting sections of the book was the part concerning his march. Everything he did, all the burning, the ransacking, and pillaging, to him was just his way to bring the war to its inevitable end. He once said, ...*When peace does come, you may call me for anything. Then will I share with you the last cracker, and watch with you to shield your homes and families against danger from every quarter.*"

"You sure seem to be a fan of his," Chris said.

"Not a fan. Just an admirer. I probably wouldn't be here today if it wasn't for him."

"Did you ever have any more contact with him?" Chris asked.

"Not directly."

Looking around, Chris asked, "Where's your son?"

Zach sat back in his chair, scratched his head, and said, "He took off last night. Back to Nashville. He insisted on going right away." Zach gave Chris a searching look. "Any idea why?"

"He thinks I'm prying. Opening up old wounds."

"He may be right. He's a good kid." He chuckled. "Almost fifty now."

Jerome came rushing into the shop. He was dripping from the rain, having come from the Lamar without an umbrella. He told Chris a telegram had just arrived. Chris thanked him and flipped him a coin.

The telegram was as terse as the previous:

Be in the boardroom 9:00 Monday morning.

"Uh oh," Chris said. "Looks like I'll be gone for a few days—back to New York. Guess they still don't like what you said about Colonel Wirz."

"When will you leave?" Zach asked.

"This is Wednesday, and they want me there Monday. Guess I'll go in the morning."

"You can catch the eastbound 8:10 to Pittsburgh," Zach said. "But I want to tell you about how lawless it was in Georgia in 'sixty-four."

When Chris left, late that afternoon, Zach gave him a book of Sherman's memoirs. He said that a lot of it was boring but it said a lot about the man, and why he did some of the things he did.

24

Near Milledgeville, Georgia, 1864

THE SOUND OF squealing hogs woke Zach the next morning. Levon was slopping their troughs, making a soft guttural sound that Zach imagined would have been a song if he could talk. Light filtered through the barn's planks, illuminating the dust in the air. The mule brayed, expecting to be fed.

Zach froze at the sound of an approaching horse. A single rider. He relaxed when he saw Levon wave at the man. The rider stopped in front of the house and dismounted, and Martha came out and greeted him. The horse was a fine looking roan. Tall, almost regal. The man wore a black jacket over a white shirt, and a black derby hat. He bowed to Martha and they talked for several minutes, then the man mounted up again and rode off at a gallop.

Martha waited for him to disappear, then walked briskly to the barn. Zach was waiting inside the door, and she told him that the man was the owner of a large farm several miles to the south, and he was warning all their neighbors that a small band of home guard ruffians had become active in the area, looking for deserters. If they suspected anyone was keeping an outlier, they would burn the house and barn and help themselves to whatever they wanted.

She looked Zach in the eye and asked, "Do we have any reason to worry?"

Zach thought a moment, "Maybe."

She was so close, he could smell her rosewater fragrance. She put her hand on his arm and Zach could feel her concern. She was not trying to judge. They agreed he would stay near the barn for the day and keep close watch, so if the guard approached, he could safely hide in there.

"I assume you can handle a gun?" she asked.

"Only if I have to."

She went back to the house and promptly returned with a Confederate Army-issued 1853 Enfield rifle. The gun was .57 caliber, made in England. Zach knew it well. It had a ladder rear sight that adjusted from a minimum of one hundred yards up to five hundred, although Zach doubted anything like pinpoint accuracy at that range. She told him that Jack had given her the gun before he left and had taught her how to use it. She also gave him a small sack that contained some Minie balls and black powder cartridges. Zach propped the gun up against the wall next to the door. He stood back and watched as it turned into a snake. Its black body was streaked in red, his eyes staring toward him, were red with narrow yellow slits, its fire-red tongue beckoning through the thick cobwebs. Zach looked away and cursed. Levon, who had been stacking hay in the corner, watched Zach's contorted face with mute understanding.

Zach busied himself inside the barn for the rest of the day. He attacked the scythe with a whetstone until he could shave the hair off his arm, the sweat dripping off his forehead, his arms aching from the repetitive motion. He took the wheels off the wagon and repacked them with grease. Midday, Levon brought him some leftover catfish and bread, and he put it aside. He pitched all the hay up to the mow and cleaned the area with a broomcorn broom. Late in the day, he finished pitching the cow manure outside, where he intended to use it in the garden. As the sun set, he opened the barn doors and felt the cool breeze on his sweat-saturated clothes.

He saw two riders coming down the lane. As they approached the house, he could see that one was a young man, slovenly dressed, with a Confederate campaign hat pulled down over his forehead. His unkempt, sand-colored hair hung to his shoulders. The other was an older man, bald, his head reflecting light from the late afternoon sun. His white beard extended down to the middle of his chest, the last few inches braided. Both had rifles pointed up in the air, the butts resting on their thighs, their fingers on the triggers.

"Hello, the house!" the older man said.

Martha came to the screen door but did not open it. Tommy peered from behind her dress and she pushed him back out of sight. The younger man dismounted and hobbled to the porch, his right foot was missing. He said something to Martha that Zach could not hear and she disappeared inside, closing the door. The older man dismounted and the two of them sat on the edge of the porch, their legs spread out in front of them. The bearded man took out a flask and both took long pulls, one wiping his mouth then taking another. The younger man whispered something, and they both cackled, sneering drunken laughter. The older slapped the other on his back and both glanced toward the door.

The air was still. The two horses munched on grass, their mouths sounding hollow as they coped with the bits in their mouths. Jake's shrill bray broke the silence, and both men looked toward the barn, as if it was the first time they had seen it. They said a few words, then Footless started toward the barn. Zach looked over at wide-eyed Levon, pointed at the haymow, and put his finger to his lips. Zach hid behind the partition leading to Jake's stall. He wanted to be ready if the man tried to start something.

The man stood in the doorway. "Nigger, you in there?" he yelled. He waited. Stone silence. "Nigger, I know you're in there. If you don't want to be on the end of a rope, stay in there and don't come out." He waited. Jake scraped the boards of his stall with his hoof. "You hear me, nigger? Mark my words or you're a dead man." He walked back to the porch, the stub of his leg swinging out with each step, his hips moving side to side.

After another pull on the flask, one man yelled to Martha to hurry up, and shortly after, she came through the door with two dishes of food. They took the dishes and Martha started back toward the door. "Your man was kilt some time ago, weren't he?" The old man said with his mouth full. "Just you and that mute nigger. Must be awful lonesome. Nice young thing like you."

The younger one snickered, "Yeah, I bet you get real lonesome. Course you got the boy. He probably takes care of you." More laughter.

Martha spun around and stalked into the house, slamming the door so hard it that sounded like a shotgun. The old man shielded his ears. "Don't know why you're upset, ma'am. Just trying to be friendly." They cleaned their plates and washed the food down with whiskey, the old man draining the last drops. They stood, picked up their rifles, and again held the barrels pointing up, fingers on the triggers.

Zach stood, looking through thin gaps in the siding. His mind raced. Levon had come down from the mow, and now made high-pitched squeals, his eyes as big as Jake's. He stood behind Zach, so close that Zach could feel his rapid breath on his back. Zach looked back, and saw Levon was shaking, his little body quivering like an aspen leaf in a breeze. Zach tried to think. If he ran at them, they would shoot him for sure. One might miss, but the other surely would not. His eyes roamed around the barn, pitchfork, shovel, rifle—no, he couldn't use it. He doubted he could even pull the trigger.

The two men went to the door Martha had just slammed. The young one stood, looking out toward the barn, and the other man yelled, "You in there, come out. We want to parley." They waited.

"Woman, get your ass out here. Leave the boy inside. If you don't, we're coming in, and you won't like what we do to him."

They waited.

"Guess we have to go in there and teach 'em a lesson," he said to the younger one.

Martha opened the door.

"Git on out here. You be nice to us, and we'll be nice to you," the bald-headed man said. Footless snickered.

Martha stepped out with a defiant look on her face, her eyes squinting, her forehead furrowed. "You lay one hand on my son and I swear I'll chop it off with a meat cleaver," she said.

"Well, well, ain't you the spunky one," the older man said. He reached down and gave her dress a hard yank. The dress tore at the waist and he gave it another jerk, ripping off the skirts. Martha slapped the old guy and turned toward the door, reaching for the handle. The other man stepped in and blocked her, holding his gun up high as he tried to embrace her. She slapped him hard and turned around so she was looking directly in his face.

Zach could see Tommy staring out the window, crying, and screaming.

The younger man took the butt of his rifle and smashed the window, yelling for the kid to shut up or he would shoot his mother. Tommy screamed louder, his sobs coming in such waves he couldn't catch his breath. The two men grabbed at Martha together and she put her arms up to guard her breasts.

Zach felt something against his back. It was Levon, with the rifle, gesturing to Zach to take it. His eyes were wild. Zach looked back toward the porch. The old man slapped Martha, throwing her against the house. Levon pushed the rifle toward Zach one more time. Zach looked at the gun, then back toward the porch, as the younger man threw Martha to the porch floor and ripped off the remainder of her dress.

Levon pushed hard with the rifle and Zach reluctantly took it, holding it away from his body. He knew the sharpshooter who had owned the gun would have it sighted-in. Levon also offered the sack with the Minie balls and powder cartridges, and Zach loaded the gun and rammed it home. He put the barrel through a gap in the barn's siding. He figured, if he shot one of the men, the other would shoot Martha or Tommy before he could reload. He sighted down the barrel toward the porch, the rifle-butt firm against his shoulder. The oiled forestock felt cold and disgusting on his left hand, like a snake's skin. His hands shook, making the rifle's sights wander, his eyes wouldn't focus.

The two men grappled with Martha, one straddling her, the other holding her legs. Zach's line of sight put Tommy several feet to the left of the men. Zach took two deep breaths. Still sighting, he waited. Levon nudged him, but he did not move.

When the younger man leaned up to say something to the other, Zach squeezed the trigger. The gun spit out the bullet with an authoritative bang and the butt recoiled hard into Zach's shoulder. The bullet tore through the back of the younger man's neck blowing a hole out the front the size of a fist. It then entered the back of the other's head, exiting his eye socket and lodging in the wall of the house, two feet from Tommy's head. Blood, bone, and brains splattered across the side of the house and both men slumped forward on top of Martha, pinning her to the floor. Zach threw the rifle across the barn into the haymow, and he and Levon charged across the barnyard to Martha.

Levon was the first one there. He picked up Martha's torn skirts and covered her near-naked torso. Zach pulled the two men off her hips and legs and threw them off the porch like the dead vermin they were. Their bodies made muffled crunching sounds as they landed on the dirt. Martha lay there, blood splattered on her bare shoulders and face. Levon used the rest of the dress to cover her up.

Zach told Levon to get a blanket and took Martha's hand with both of his, "Martha?" he whispered. Her left cheek was bruised and already starting to swell. It was hard to tell if the blood she was covered in was hers or her assailant's. She nodded, she was okay, and looked into Zach's eyes. Tommy came close and Martha held him tight with one hand, the other still holding Zach's. When Levon arrived with the blanket, Zach stood up and looked the other way as Martha covered herself. He looked at the dead men, then back to the blood-spattered wall, and knew it was all his fault.

Darkness settled in as Martha went inside, clutching the blanket around her. Zach told Levon to hitch up the wagon. They would have to dispose of the men's bodies.

After checking on Martha, Zach loaded the bodies into the wagon, along with two shovels. He told Levon to fetch the rifle, and the two of them drove toward the river with the dead men's horses in tow. Near the river, they found an area of sandy loam where Zach outlined with a shovel the grave for the two men. Then he outlined another larger area and explained to Levon that they had to get rid of the dead men's horses, too. If they didn't, others might come looking and accuse them of murder.

Zach dug the larger grave while Levon worked on the smaller. The shovel handle creaked with each large shovelful. Stopping occasionally for a drink of water from the river, they worked in silence.

Zach finally finished and helped Levon. When the grave was deep enough, Zach threw the two men's bodies into the hole and they covered them up with dirt.

"Now comes the hard part," Zach said.

He led one of the horses to the edge of the larger grave and gave the reins to Levon. He went back to the wagon and made sure the other horse was tied securely, then took the rifle, checked it, and told Levon to look away. He aimed the gun just behind the horse's ear and fired. The horse slumped and fell into the hole. They did the same with the second horse.

Long after midnight, Levon reined the mule up in front of the barn. They had taken a brief swim in the river and were still wet but refreshed. The barn had been closed, and retained the day's heat, so Zach opened all the doors and lay down on the straw. With his hands behind his head, he tried to recount the day, but when he got to the two men on the porch, he didn't want to think about it.

The air was humid and the night breeze stiffened, portending a change in the weather. Zach thought about what he should do. Martha and Tommy might not get through the winter without him, but his presence on the farm endangered them. He thought about where the two men had come from and remembered the neighbor's warning, but he had said the guard was a group of men, not just two. How many, he didn't know. He wondered about Sherman, and when the war would be over. It had been more than four years since it started, and from what he had seen and heard, the South might not last much longer. Maybe then, he could get the farm back in good enough shape for him to go home to Tennessee. But then, there was Martha.

Zach heard a rustling in the hay on the floor, soft footsteps coming toward him. It was Tommy. Without a word, Tommy lay down beside him, put his little arm across his chest, and went to sleep. His breathing was soft and even, his warm body snuggled up tight. Zach remembered going on two- or three-day fishing trips with his father, just the two of them. They used to go every summer, on a different river each time. His father's steady hand always guiding him, but also letting him make a few mistakes.

A light approached from the house. It was Martha looking for Tommy. Her robe brushed the top of the scattered hay as she came near. When she saw the two of them together in the hay, she sighed with obvious relief. Zach put his finger to his lips and saw a smile in her eyes. The light from her lantern illuminated her face, its glow shrouded by her long hair, which hung to her waist, untethered. He inhaled her scent as she kneeled down next to Tommy and kissed him on the forehead. She was carrying a light blanket, which she spread over both of them, tucking it in around Tommy. She hesitated then leaned over and kissed Zach full on the lips, her hair falling softly on his face. She lingered there for a few seconds, her face only inches from his. She ran her finger lightly over his scar, mouthed the words, "thank you," and left, her lantern light disappearing into the darkness.

25

New York City, New York, 1908

Leaving the Hudson River ferry, Chris fought his way through the weary throngs of workers leaving the city for the weekend. He had sent a telegram to Sarah to meet him, and he looked for her among the rows of shivering onlookers. A cold front had moved through during the day, dropping the temperature into the twenties, and most of the travelers were unprepared, including Chris.

Sarah's favorite color was any shade of yellow, and Chris caught sight of her bright lemon scarf, like a pinpoint of light amidst the drab gray of winter. Her face radiated joy when their eyes met.

They rode the streetcar uptown to their apartment. Two years prior, they had met at a book fair, where Sarah was promoting her latest book: *The Making of Jane.* The book, which she considered her best work so far, was a caricature of the maturation of a young girl and how her character was formed. Critics compared her book to *Jane Eyre,* and many recognized that Sarah might have been writing about her own experiences growing up.

Sarah was a fierce believer in women's rights. She was the daughter of Stephen Elliott, who had been bishop of the Protestant Episcopal Church during the war. His church was located in Milledgeville, the then capital of Georgia.

———

The apartment was warm and cozy. Chris bathed, washing off two days of travel grime, while Sarah made his favorite dinner, chicken fried steak.

As she busied herself at the stove, Chris came up behind her and switched off the gas. Dressed in his bathrobe, he put his arms around her and whispered, "Even though I'm hungry as a horse, it can wait a while longer." He nipped at her ear. She turned to him and they embraced, and he lifted her up and took her to the bedroom.

Later, still enjoying the comfort of their bed, she asked him what he intended to say to Pulitzer. Chris replied that if Pulitzer wanted him to change his story about Wirz, then he might have to find another job. He was unwilling to change the story just because an editor didn't want to hurt his paper's circulation and diminish advertising revenue.

"Your story has captivated New York," Sarah said later at supper. "Everybody is anxious to find out what happens to Zach. It's better than reading a book."

"Pulitzer was right about one thing. The North is ready to start talking about the war again," Chris said.

"Yes, but are they willing to accept that the South had the right to leave the Union? And that they preyed upon women and children, leaving them destitute? I just don't get it," she said, moving her food from one side of her plate to the other. "Seems like yellow journalism to me."

"You don't think Zach's story is yellow journalism, do you?" Chris asked.

"Didn't say exactly that. Your story has revealed the truth about Colonel Wirz, and you even pointed out the Northern prisons were as bad, if not worse. However, you seem to be getting a soft spot for Sherman, the butcher of the South."

"You understand that I only write what Zach tells me," Chris said.

"You're writing some things that we both know aren't really true. Regardless of what Zach says."

"My research says otherwise," Chris said. "On the train ride back, I read some surprising things about Sherman. I learned that at West Point, he fell for a young girl, Cecilia Stovall, who was the sister of his roommate. She wouldn't have him, and later married another man by the name of Shelman. They lived in Cass County, Georgia, near where I was born.

When Sherman came through the area, just before the Battle of Atlanta, he found out she lived there, and set up guards around her house so nobody would bother her. He left her a note that said, 'Forgive me, I am only a soldier.'"

Sarah glared. "This is going nowhere," she said, and got up and cleared the table.

"You wash, I'll dry," Chris whispered.

———

The elevator to the top floor of *New York World* building took almost two minutes. Joseph Pulitzer had built the tallest building in the world to house his newspaper, and now, as he sat behind his desk, Chris thought he looked like a self-appointed lord of the realm. His office doubled as *The World's* boardroom, with his desk at one end of a long table with twelve chairs.

"Martin. So good to see you again," Pulitzer said offering Chris his hand. He motioned Chris to a chair and introduced him to the editor, Frank Cobb, and ex-reporter, Nellie Bly. Even though Chris had met Pulitzer just one time before, Pulitzer acted like they were longtime friends. Chris sat down, feeling uneasy. He could understand why Pulitzer and Cobb were at the table, but why Nellie Bly? She was a renowned investigative journalist, and only a few years before had traveled around the world in 72 days as a publicity stunt. Chris could think of only one reason she was at the meeting and his anxiety grew.

Chris sat and listened to Pulitzer talk about the paper's new circulation numbers, which were well over one million daily. He said he thought the numbers could double if he could get enough publicity, and he expounded on his ideas to accomplish that.

"Which brings us to your story," he said finally. "You have captivated this city. Everyone wonders what will happen to Zach Harkin next. I must admit that when your installments are printed, our daily sales rate increases. The last episode, with those two lawless ruffians, caused our sales to increase over twenty percent."

"Which brings us back to why we wanted to talk to you," said Cobb.

"Yes. We're worried about the impression you have left with our readers about Colonel Wirz," Pulitzer said. "We citizens of the North truly believe Wirz was a lowdown scoundrel, and your reports that he was not responsible for the horrible treatment at Andersonville have turned the stomachs of many of our readers. Remember why we print newspapers, Mister Martin. We want to sell them. We want to tell the readers what they want to hear so they will buy more papers. We don't want to alienate our good clientele with half-truths and maybes just to make an obscure, if not false, impression. The customer is king, Mister Martin."

Chris removed his glasses and rubbed his temples. He leaned forward with his elbows on the table and looked directly at Pulitzer. "What are you saying to me, Mister Pulitzer? Do you want me to retract the parts about Wirz not being able to feed his prisoners and provide them with clothing and shelter? Do you want me to fabricate this story? To distort the truth?"

"Well, I..."

"I can only write what I am told. Zach Harkin's story is very personal. It's his story. The first time it's ever been told. I can't just unilaterally change something because I, or you, think it would be better for business to do so." He glanced over at Bly. She was looking at Pulitzer.

"We're not asking you to 'change the story,'" Cobb said. "We just want you to soften it up a bit."

"Are you giving me a choice?" said Chris.

Pulitzer stood. "Yes we are. And the choice is yours." He left the room.

"What the hell did he mean by that?" Chris asked Cobb.

Without Pulitzer in the room, Cobb softened. "Mister Pulitzer is used to getting his way."

"And I am not used to fabrication."

"Nobody's asking for you to 'fabricate,' Martin. You know this business. It's either grow or die. Just look at the numbers *The World* has attained in the last five years. Pulitzer is a master journalist. He has instincts that nobody else has, and that includes Bill Hearst over at the *Journal*."

Chris took out his glasses and cleaned them with his handkerchief. He leaned forward in his chair and pointed to the portrait of Pulitzer behind his desk. "That man does not intimidate me one bit, Cobb. I am first a journalist, and to me that means I don't 'change' stories just to please readership. I write the truth, and if the truth doesn't fit into this paper, then you need another man." Chris stood.

Cobb remained seated. "He won't like it," Cobb warned.

Chris went toward the door. "Imagine this headline in the *New York Journal: 'World* fires reporter for telling the truth.'"

"You wouldn't dare," Cobb said, jumping to his feet.

"You tell Pulitzer the choice is his, not mine," Chris said. "And, by the way, you tell him I didn't miss his little trick of asking Nellie Bly to attend the meeting. If he wants to give her my story, she can have it." He walked out through the open door.

————

Chris had agreed with Sarah that they would meet for lunch at Delmonico's in Lower Manhattan. He was early, but Sarah had already arrived and was seated at a table near a window. As he approached, she was staring out the window, even though it was covered with a lace curtain.

"Hi, honey. You're early," Chris said, sitting down.

"I've been here a while. Just thinking."

"Thinking about what?"

"Thinking about you, I guess. How did it go?" She had a faint smile. She normally wore her hair down, but today she had it pinned up. Chris liked it that way. It exposed her long, graceful neck. The white collar of her green taffeta dress was ruffled and accentuated her face. Chris thought she looked as beautiful as he had ever seen her.

"Not well. Pulitzer and Cobb are really digging in on this. I suspect Cobb is just following orders, but it is clear that if I want to keep my job at *The World*, I will have to modify the story."

"That shouldn't be much of a problem, should it?" she asked.

The waiter brought them menus. They both ordered poached salmon.

Sarah had her right hand on her water glass, turning it slowly. "You're going to make the changes, aren't you?"

"Well…"

"It's not like you have a bunch of other offers out there," she added. "You're about to break out. This Harkin story has been wonderful for you. Everybody is talking about it."

"The idea that somebody can insist that I change a story to meet somebody else's expectations is abhorrent to me, Sarah. I'm not sure I could live with myself if I did it."

Sarah stared at her glass. "This is all about Wirz, isn't it? Some lowly Confederate colonel who may have been misunderstood. So what? Why would you put your job in jeopardy for such a small point?"

"I consider the truth to be more than just a 'small point,' Sarah."

The salmon was served, but the conversation remained stilted. They discussed Sarah's book, and her meeting later that day with a new publisher.

Sarah stared out the window. Chris knew she was working up to say something, so he gave her time. Her finger went to the rim of her glass and she slowly moved it around the edge. Finally, she said, "You're not going to change what you wrote about Sherman either, are you?"

Chris took a deep breath. He knew the question was coming, but he still wasn't ready for it.

"My granddaddy and my daddy both swore that Sherman was there when his men sacked Milledgeville. Surely you cannot ask me to believe your hero Harkin over my own flesh and blood. You wouldn't ask me to do that, would you?"

"And, as a reporter, I cannot change Harkin's story. You wouldn't ask me to do that either."

They stared at each other. Her jaw was set, her nostrils flared.

She broke their gaze, looking at the clock. "Oh my, I'm late," she said. She got up and left.

That evening, the subject was not mentioned. Chris left for Knoxville early the next morning.

26

Milledgeville, Georgia, 1864

ORNING DEW CLUNG to the scythe as Zach pulled it through the heavy clover. The sun shone red through moisture-laden clouds. He wanted to finish the field before the rain came. The clover would be the feedstock mainstay through the winter for the animals. Three days had passed since they had buried the two men, and Zach needed to get the hay in the barn before the clover went to seed. The situation was urgent enough that he was willing to risk being seen.

He stopped and rested his arms on the scythe handle; he was almost finished.

One of the pigs squealed in the pen next to the barn. A high-pitched, frightened sound. His line of sight was obstructed by the barn, so he dropped his scythe and ran to get a better view. The first thing he saw was four riderless horses and a wagon with a team in front of the house. Martha stood on the back stoop, holding her head in her hands. He counted four soldiers in faded blue uniforms. Two were in the pigpen and two were on the front porch. They all carried side arms.

A shot rang out and the squealing stopped. The two men in the pen converged on the body of a pig, one wielding a butcher knife. Another man chased chickens, and the fourth went into the house. Zach saw that the side of the wagon was marked "US."

The two men in the pigpen started to chase a second pig, which ran around the pen squealing louder than the first. The pig was fast, and the men couldn't get a good shot. They tried to corner it. One dove at it, but it managed to slip away. When the man got up, his uniform was covered with mud. The other man laughed, then shot the pig as it cowered in a corner.

A man came out of the house carrying pots and pans. Levon approached Zach from the rear, same as before, carrying the rifle, urging Zach to take it. Zach put up his hand and mouthed "No." He had no chance against five armed soldiers, and shooting one or maybe two would gain them nothing but the end of a rope.

When Martha heard the second shot, she must have realized she would have no pork for the winter, she said, "That's all the pork we have. You can't take everything."

"Call it the Yankee version of impressment," one of the men said curtly. "Bet none of you Southern belles said anything when Johnny Reb came knocking and took your crops, your slaves, and everything else he wanted."

"But we can't get through the winter without meat. You can't leave us to starve."

The man ignored her and went back into the house for more.

When the two men started to drag the second pig toward the wagon, Martha ran to stop them. She stood directly in their way. "Please leave us one. Just one. You don't need both. Please."

They pulled the pig around her and threw it into the wagon. She held her arms out toward the men, pleading. Her face was flushed and tears poured down her cheeks.

Watching all of this from his hidden position in the barn, Zach felt helpless.

One of the men, who appeared to be in charge, walked up to her, his uniform bloody, his boots covered with pig offal, and asked her where her husband was. She told him he had been killed at Chancellorsville, which seemed to satisfy him. "We'll leave you with your cow and mule," he said. "The cow's too skinny and we have enough mules."

The soldiers mounted and the wagon pulled away, disappearing down the lane, and the clouds let loose a downpour. Martha went into the house and Zach ran the short distance to the porch. He called her name.

She came to the door, her eyes red, her cheeks streaked with tears. She looked up at him through the screen, "How will we get through the winter?" she said.

He opened the screen and she came into his arms, burying her head in his chest, sobbing. He pulled her close. Tommy came out and hugged their legs. Zach thought about their options and abruptly excused himself, heading back toward the barn. He told Levon to harness Jake to the wagon.

Shortly, and without saying a word, he drove off down the lane, the rain coming down in sheets, the wagon wheels leaving mud tracks in the already muddy red soil.

The tracks from the Union wagon headed south from the end of the lane toward where Zach assumed was Milledgeville. He was no more than ten minutes behind them and he urged Jake on at a good trot. As he approached town, the tracks were lost in a mire of many others. He crested a rise and saw the town below, the capital of Georgia. A huge column of smoke rose from the city center and other smaller fires burned nearby. Union soldiers were everywhere. A large three-story structure blazed in the town square. It was the penitentiary, which had been converted to an arsenal by the Confederacy. Wagons and horses blocked the main street. Zach stopped the wagon in front of an Episcopal church, just off the square. The church's roof was caved in, and a curious sweet odor emanated from within.

Several of the wagons were marked "XX Corps" and Zach assumed they were part of Sherman's army. Nobody paid much attention to him as he walked up the street toward a crowd of soldiers listening to a general, giving orders. Zach asked a soldier who was speaking.

"General Henry Warren Slocum," the man answered, as a cheer went up from the crowd. "Some of us call him 'Slow come' since he was so slow showing up at Gettysburg."

The general motioned for the crowd to calm down. He was tall, slim, and clean-shaven, but for a neat mustache. He went on to tell the men that they would move out at first light, toward Savannah, and by that time the war might be over and they all could go home. Another loud cheer. Several officers stood behind the general. Zach thought they might be his aides, so he worked his way over to them.

He tapped one on the shoulder, "Excuse me, sir, do you have a minute?"

The aide looked him up and down, seemingly surprised at being approached by a civilian, or at least a soldier without a uniform. "I don't have a minute, so make it thirty seconds," the officer said.

Zach told him he was with the S.S. Service and gave him the note Sherman had given him outside of Atlanta. The officer read it, looked up at Zach, and said, "So what? What has this to do with the General?"

Zach explained that he was living at a small farm just a few miles north of Milledgeville. He told the man about the Union soldiers taking all their food for the winter. "I want it back," Zach said flatly.

The officer smiled, seemingly amused by this brazen young man demanding his food back. The general had finished his speech and the aide excused himself to Zach and showed Sherman's note to him, whispering in his ear. The general looked over at Zach, then reread the note. He took the note, turned it over, and jotted something on the back. The aide returned, handed Zach the note, and told him to go down by the river where the food was being stockpiled and to give the note to any officer he saw. Zach thanked him and went back to the wagon. He flipped the note over, shielding it from the rain, and read, "Give this guy his goddamned food back," signed, General H.W. Slocum.

27

Milledgeville, Georgia 1864

THE RAIN WAS letting up and the sky was brightening to the west as Zach yelled "gee" to Jake turning left onto the lane that led to Martha's farm. The wet reins felt heavy in Zach's hands. Zach was soaked to the skin and cold, he could feel winter in the crisp air. The wagon weighing three to four hundred pounds more than when he left, carved deep ruts in the sodden soil. White smoke columned upward from Martha's stove. To Zach, it felt like coming home.

General Slocum's quartermaster was a short, fat and jolly. The kind of man who was happy when his stomach was full but mean and ugly when food was not in ample supply. Luckily, when Zach presented the note to him, he had already eaten his fill. Foraging wagons had arrived earlier laden with beef, pork and grains from the farms in the area. He was in a generous mood.

He asked Zach if he saw the wagon that had been to his farm and Zach replied that there were so many he could not tell. The makeshift stocking area was beside the river, surrounded hundreds of negroes, waiting for something to eat. Slaughtered hogs and cattle were piled in a long row. All under the cover of large tarpaulins. Freight wagons laden with wheat and corn stood nearby, ready to pull out to be distributed to the army. The quartermaster looked at Zach's little wagon and mule, smiled, and told him to take no more than he could carry. Zach, not being able to believe his good fortune, wasted no time grabbing two nice hog carcasses, two sides of beef, a sack of oats, another of corn and a bag of salt.

Martha and Tommy were waiting on the porch as Zach jumped off the wagon, a big smile on his face. "Come see what I got," He said proudly. "We have some salting to do."

Levon approached from the barn and excitedly stood up on a wheel axle to see over the wagon's side boards. When he saw what was there his face lit up with a smile from ear to ear, his head shaking up and down making excited guttural sounds. Zach lifted Tommy up so he could see and Martha peered in on her tip toes both looking with wide eyed wonderment.

"This should get us through the winter," Zach said.

Zach and Levon hung the meat up in the barn from the biggest barn beam and after a thorough drying, got to work salting it down. When they were nearly done, Tommy came in with a clean pair of britches and shirt, "M-Mommy said you would like some dry c-clothes," he said. "These were my father's. She wants you to come to dinner."

"Thank you, young fella," Zach said, ruffling Tommy's hair.

"You'll c-come?"

"How could I refuse your mother's cooking?" Zach asked.

Dressed in the clean, dry clothes, Zach stepped up on the rear stoop and washed his hands and face in the basin. He caught the aroma of cooking beef wafting through the screen door and his mouth watered. "Something smells mighty good," he said, peering in.

Martha wiped her hands on her apron and greeted him at the door with a warm smile. Her face was flushed from the heat of the stove which to Zach made her look even more beautiful. Her cotton dress was trimmed in white lace outlining the V-shaped neckline which stressed her trim figure. The skirt was full and extended to her ankles and Zach noticed she was barefoot.

"Hope you like pot roast," she said offering Zach a chair at the table. She called Tommy who sat next to Zach, across from Martha's chair. His dark hair was parted and combed over revealing the same high forehead as his mother's.

"Ma'am, pot roast is my favorite, ma'am. How did you know?"

"Woman's intuition, maybe," she said. "By the way, please call me 'Marta', 'Martha' seems so formal."

While Marta took the roast out of the oven Zach reported that the beef and pork was nearly all salted down and Levon was finishing the job in the barn. They would put it down in the fruit cellar in the morning. Her arm brushed his as she served his plate loaded with meat, potatoes and vegetables, and her warmth spread through him. Just her near presence, her touch, the surroundings, the aromas, the supper table—he felt like he was home. He looked at his shirt, the last person to wear it was the man whose jaw he had shot off. He felt like an imposter, even though he had never lied to Marta, he hadn't been truthful either. He stared at the pendulum of the clock on the wall.

"Ahem. Thinking about home?" she asked.

"I was just thinking how happy I am," he said. He told them about all of the Negroes in town, down by the river. How they were standing around by the hundreds waiting for the army to feed them. Zach guessed that the soldiers had freed them as they marched through and then he asked about Levon, and Marta explained that when they were married, Jack had insisted on giving Levon his freedom. Levon had decided to stay on after that, and they paid him a small amount for the work he did.

"Jack must have been quite a guy," Zach said.

"M-mom made peach cobbler," Tommy said.

"Also my favorite," Zach said smiling at her.

Marta started clearing the supper dishes and Zach jumped to help. She put her hand on his shoulder and pushed him back into his chair. "You've done enough, today," she said warmly.

She served the cobbler again lightly touching Zach arm. When the meal was over Marta told Tommy it was time for bed and after a little complaining, kissed his mom goodnight and padded off to his room. Halfway there he turned around ran back to Zach and put his arms around him, squeezed tight, then without another word, Tommy went to bed.

"Sometimes actions are better than words," Marta said.

Sitting next to Zach she put both her hands on Zach's, "You have saved us," she said. Her touch was soft and warm, then she traced the outline of the scar on his face looking into his eyes. "Did you get this in the war?"

"Andersonville." He ran the back of his fingers over the back of her hand.

"Somebody waiting for you at home?" she asked.

"No." He said softly.

Marta got up from the table and walked to her bedroom leaving the door half open. Zach looked at the door and wondered if he had said something wrong. The fire in the stove cast flickering shadows on the kitchen walls. He put his hands up to his face, Marta fragrance was still there. Even though he had just eaten, he felt a hollowness in his stomach like an ache, a confused, anxious emptiness.

Then she appeared behind the half open door. She was wearing a floor-length night robe tied at the waist. Her hair hung down touching her shoulders, framing her cheeks as the light played on her face. Zach thought she looked a little like a ghost but more like a dream. She slipped the robe off her shoulders exposing her breasts. Not saying a word, with a coquettish smile she slowly turned to go letting the robe fall onto the floor. He followed her into the room. She was sitting on the edge of the bed and he went to her.

She helped him with his clothes, "Please be patient," she said softly. "Its been almost four years."

He unbuttoned his shirt, "Much more than that for me," he said.

"I thought so," she said.

Trying to remove his britches, Zach almost fell, his free foot thumping hollow on the wood floor.

She smiled. Her manner was relaxed and eased his tension. For a while the pain of the war floated away like an eagle caught in a late afternoon updraft, soaring higher and higher.

28

CHRIS LEANED FORWARD in his chair looking directly at Zach. "You said you saw an Episcopal church in Milledgeville. Did you happen to notice the name?"

"Saint Stephen's. I remember because we have a Saint Stephen's Church here in Knoxville."

"And you said the roof was caved in?" Chris asked.

"Yes."

"Some have said that the church was blown up by the Yankees," Chris said.

"Didn't appear that way," Zach said. "An arsenal next door had blown up, and debris from the explosion landed on the church roof, causing it to cave in."

"And you said you smelled a peculiar order?"

"Yes. I think it was molasses. They poured it down the organ pipes to cripple their ability to hold services. The Episcopal Church had almost universally backed the Southern cause, and many Union troops, who might have been Episcopalian themselves, took exception."

Chris leaned back in his chair. He had arrived back in Knoxville late the night before. Back in New York, Pulitzer had called his bluff. Chris felt like he had been put into a corner with no good options. He got up to fill his coffee cup for the third time. Zach waited for him to speak.

"Did you see Sherman when you were in Milledgeville?" Chris asked.

"No. I heard he was about twenty miles south. The Union army was in Milledgeville for only one day and one night. Then they moved out, heading east again."

"Are you sure?" Chris asked.

"About as sure as I can be," Zach said. "Why?"

"The war has been over for more than fifty years, Zach. But, many people still have strong feelings. I guess the old saying 'time heals all wounds' doesn't apply."

Zach's face sagged. "So many wounds," he said softly.

29

Milledgeville, Georgia, 1864

B Y LATE MORNING, the sun had burned off the low-lying fog. The air was fresh and dry, with a slight breeze from the west. The high-pitched calls of migrating geese heralded the coming winter.

Zach took a hayfork out of the mow. Levon came into the barn and picked up Zach's still-wet clothes. He pointed toward the house and moved his hands as if using a washboard. Zach nodded, walked out to the field, and starting on the far end, tedded the hay so the sun would dry it out faster. He could feel the stubble of the cut clover through the soles of his shoes, hearing the stiff stems crunch as he walked. He was sorry he had cut the clover the previous day, as the rain would cause it to rot if it didn't dry quickly enough.

He thought about removing a stand of trees on the edge of the property to increase the number of plantable acres. With those acres cleared, he could plant more corn and beans, sell them, and buy a team of horses. He would paint the barn; add a larger corncrib.

He had awakened early that morning in Martha's bed, their bodies still naked, his arms still around her. He had wanted to wake her, to make love again, to stay there forever. He had lain there unmoving, inhaling her. The pure joy of her was unlike anything he had ever experienced. As the first light of the new day showed a vague grayness through the window, he had quietly risen, donned his clothes, and left. He would tell her the truth at supper.

By mid-afternoon, Zach had finished tedding the hay once and had started to turn it over again. He planned to take it up the next afternoon. He would pitch it on the wagon and haul it to the barn, where he would pitch it up to the mow. Levon had brought him water around noon, but he realized he had not eaten all day. As he worked the field toward the barn and farmhouse, with each sweep of the fork, he glanced up to look for Martha. He didn't know if the ache in his belly was caused by hunger or something else.

The sun was low on the horizon when Zach finished the second round. He was satisfied the hay could be harvested the next morning, after the dew burned off. He went to the barn and saw Levon in his corner, eating his supper. The ache worsened. Levon was more animated than usual. He kept pointing toward the house then wrinkling his face up, wiping his hands across his eyes. Zach went to the house.

The back door was closed. He knocked. He heard Tommy's little feet running toward the door, but when he got there, he heard Martha tell him to go to his room. The ache in Zach's belly became a lump in his throat. Somehow, he thought, she must know.

He waited a few moments, then lightly tapped the door again with the back of his knuckle. No response. His heart pounded, his forehead beaded with sweat, and his hands shook. He sat on the back stoop. He remembered his school history class, when they talked about French guillotines and how the poor, feckless victim would place his neck at the bottom and wait for the blade to fall. He felt that way. He knew, however, that whatever the coming punishment was, he deserved it. His fear turned to sorrow. He buried his head in his hands and wept.

Minutes later, the door opened, "You know the difference between just a plain Yankee and a goddamned Yankee?" Martha asked.

Zach turned to face her. Her lips were pursed tight, her face was red, her eyes bloodshot. He could only stare.

"A Yankee is just a robber and murderer; a goddamned Yankee is a robber and murderer who is also a goddamned liar." She opened the door and threw his still-damp clothes at him, then she threw Sherman's note, all wadded up. It hit him in the face. "I want you off my farm. Now get out of here. I never want to see you again. Ever." Her forehead was furrowed, her eyes only slits. She slammed the door so hard the side of the house shook.

Sherman's note had hit him on the cheek, and though it was only paper, the effect was like a twenty-pound sledgehammer. He cursed himself for not having told her earlier. He felt like he had betrayed her. Guilt flooded over him. His mind slowed almost to a stop.

"Could I please tell my side of the story?" he asked, loud enough for her to hear through the door. He waited, but she did not answer. His legs felt weak. He sat on the edge of the stoop and forced himself to breathe, to think.

An hour later, he yelled into the house, "I will sit here until you hear me out…" He heard her close her bedroom door.

The frosty moon played hide and seek amongst the scattered clouds as the temperature dropped through the night. Mars, a dirty red, dipped down to the level of the trees by the river, slipping out of sight. The cool air penetrated Zach's shirt. The planks on the stoop offered little comfort. A coyote howled in the distance, a long, mournful wail. Zach waited.

He thought about home, his mother and father, helping in the gun shop, working with the guns. He had been proud of the way he could shoot. Holding a gun had been almost instinctive for him.

Then the war. Shiloh. Shooting Johnston. Taking out a whole battery of Rebel cannon. All seemed natural. The right thing to do. Then the Rebel sharpshooter. Jack. Martha's husband. His jaw blown away. The sickening sound of a bullet hitting flesh and bone. Seeing him up close, the blood and bones splattered against a tree. If only he had missed, everything would be different. Then again, he never would have met Martha. But was it worth it? He traced the scar on his face, remembering her touch, her soft hands, her fragrance. Yes, it was worth it.

As the first light of morning wove its way through the cottonwoods, Zach stood, his body stiff and cold. He moved his hands and arms back and forth and walked in tight circles to get his blood flowing. Hunger pangs reminded him he had not eaten since the previous morning. Jake brayed from the barn. The rooster crowed.

Zach sat on the stoop, facing away from the kitchen door. He could hear soft footsteps from inside as Martha moved about. He heard her come to the door, probably to see if he was still there. Then the sound of dishes as she took them off the drying rack and placed them on the shelves.

The sun rose above the trees. The sunflowers in the garden opened and turned toward the east.

"Martha, if you won't come out here and talk to me, then I will tell you my story from here. If you care at all, please hear me out," Zach said.

"I grew up in Knoxville, Tennessee, where my father was a gunsmith. He gave me my first rifle when I was nine and I spent a lot of time hunting and shooting." Zach told her the complete story of his childhood and how he signed up for the war, then went to Shiloh, then joined the U.S. Sharpshooters.

"One morning, while we were hunkered down, a good friend of mine was shot by someone we later found out was a Rebel sharpshooter."

The rattling of dishes stopped.

"The shot came from over three hundred yards away, on the other side of the river, and we all thought we were under siege. Hiding behind logs, we would expose somebody's campaign cap on a stick and it would instantly have a hole in it. We realized the Rebel sharpshooter was one of the best we had ever come up against. We could not see him, nor did we know exactly where he was hiding. I was selected to swim across the river at night and find him in the morning. The river was dark and dangerous, but I followed my lieutenant's orders.

The next morning I did something that I have deeply regretted ever since. Not a day goes by that I don't see your husband sitting on the end of my bed, haunting me."

Zach heard soft sobs from inside. He waited a few moments.

"The images of the killing affected me and I could not continue as a soldier, so I was mustered out and sent back to Knoxville. At home, I still could not sleep. The dead man's family was in my mind like a black shadow, always there. I decided the only way I could find peace would be to find the dead man's family and try to make amends. I had no idea who or where, but I had to try."

Jake brayed in the barn. Levon was behind in his chores.

Zach continued telling how he left home, was taken prisoner, eventually found Susie McGowan and her.

"Then I was caught in a whirlwind of my own doing," he continued. "I loved you and thought if I told you the truth you would throw me out. Discard me like an old dishrag. Several times, I wanted to tell you, but my fear of losing you prevailed.

Now you know. I put myself at your mercy. If you ask me to go, I will. I want to stay. I want to stay with you and Tommy. I will go to the barn now. A lot of things need to be done around here and Levon can't handle them alone. Please think about what I told you and remember I love you more than anything."

Zach was sure she had heard everything he said, but she had not spoken a word to him, only her soft sobs, which he could still hear as he walked to the barn. He felt naked. He had told her everything. She was the only person on Earth who knew his whole story, and he had the strange sensation that he felt even closer to her now that she knew. She would decide.

30

Near Milledgeville, Georgia, 1864

OVER THE NEXT several days, Zach worked from first light in the morning to well after sundown, putting up the hay, tilling the garden, repairing fences, whatever he could find that needed doing.

He started to clear the trees in the far corner of the farm, near the river. Levon helped crosscut the fallen trees into firewood lengths, which he would then split for the next winter. Although pulling the saw through a log was beyond his strength, Levon could keep it straight while Zach supplied the muscle.

Sometimes Zach would catch a glimpse of Martha as she hung out the wash or fetched water from the well. Her head was always down. She never acknowledged his presence. In the sun, she wore a bonnet pulled down low. From a distance, he could not see her face. She wore cotton dresses that would brush over the grass as she walked, always tight around the waist. Her outright dismissal of his presence was painful, but Zach found solace in the hard work. At night, when he finally crawled into his nest in the haymow, he found sleep easier when he was totally exhausted.

When he and Levon returned to the barn each night, Levon would share his supper. Each evening, Martha would place one plate of food on the manger shelf, with a towel over it to keep the flies away. There always seemed to be enough for the two of them, and Zach latched onto the thought that she had increased the amount for him.

Late one afternoon, Levon and Zach had cut down the last cottonwood in the new field and were bucking it clean, preparing to cut the main log into pieces of firewood size. The sky was gray, but an opening appeared on the western horizon, allowing the sun to burst through, outlining the clouds in a fiery red. Zach rested his crosscut saw on end and wiped his brow, wondering if it was a good sign or bad.

Movement along the river drew his attention. Two black men were making their way along the bank, trying to stay hidden in the bordering brush and trees. They moved forward as if they feared being followed, ducking low, keeping out of sight as much as possible. When Zach pointed them out, Levon seemed to recognize them. He grinned and waved his arms, trying to get their attention. The two men saw him, but stayed in the trees. Levon ran toward them, his little legs picking their way through the dead tree limbs. When he reached them, all three embraced.

The Negroes were tall, muscular, and middle aged. They wore identical shirts and britches. The clothes were torn and caked with mud. They still seemed reluctant to come out from the cover of the trees, so Zach walked over to them, moving slowly, so they wouldn't feel threatened.

"We don't want no trouble, Massa," one said, with his hands extended out as if he was trying to hide behind them.

Levon tried to reassure the two, and they gradually relaxed, breaking out in big smiles, obviously happy to see Levon. All four sat on a log, and one of them started to talk. He pointed to Levon, looked at Zach, and said, "Mufa, me, and him," he pointed to the other man, "are brothers." He explained that all three had worked for 'the Missus' father and that he had given Mufa to the Missus a long time ago. She had renamed him Levon, and they hadn't seen him since.

The two men spoke in broken English. Zach could not understand all of what they said, but he did learn that the plantation where they had worked had been burned to the ground, all the crops, barns, sheds, main house, everything. The hungry "soldier men" with blue uniforms rode in one day and told them that from that day on all slaves were free. The "Massah" of the house was taken away, leaving all the slaves on their own. The soldiers rode off and left them with nothing but the clothes on their backs. Luckily, the soldiers hadn't found the outside cellar, which was loaded with potatoes, salted pork, and apples. The freed slaves had been living off the contents of the cellar ever since. Other freed slaves had stopped by on their way north and told them that Milledgeville was infested with lawless gangs of home guard, homeless soldiers, and Northern shysters roaming around stealing, raping, lynching, and shooting. The two men said that they had to hide every time someone rode in, and the only thing they could think to do was get as far north as they could before the winter. They were told the gangs might shoot ex-slaves on sight, so they tried to stay hidden.

As night approached, a cool breeze picked up from the west, and Zach asked the two if they would like to spend the night in the barn. They eagerly accepted, picking up the burlap sacks they were carrying and following him. One held up his sack and told them they could feast on pork and potatoes. It was too heavy, he said. They all laughed.

As the two black men were making nests in the hay, one said, to no one in particular, "Shur is harder than the massa's bed, but shur more better." He laughed.

Zach looked at the two men in wonderment. They had lost their African home and family, were enslaved, then lost the only way of life they knew in America. They were without shelter or a long-term supply of food, and were being pursued by lawless men who might kill them for the fun of it, but they were happy.

Under the dim light of a lantern, Zach eased back in his own nest and took a bite of a big sweet potato. The potato had probably been cooked on hot embers from a mature fire. The skin was dark brown and crusty. The combination of the smoky flavor and the moistness on the inside was very agreeable. Although Zach had seen slaves before, he had never spent much time with them. These ex-slaves were the first Zach had ever actually spoken to at any length.

He remembered his father and mother talking about the inhumanity of slavery and how wrong it was that human beings could be subjugated to another person's use.

These men were real. He liked them. Even though they had lost their free- dom, they were generous, and had a strong sense of family. They clearly loved their brother, Mufa. He wondered why other people hated them so. Why would they indiscriminately kill these men? Were they some kind of threat? Or was it just some kind of perverted sport?

Zach felt the coolness of the night air seeping through the cracks in the barn siding and wrapped the waxed blanket around himself, nestling down to smooth over the hay stubble he could feel through his clothes. He thought about Martha and wondered if she had seen the two black men before they entered the barn. She had freed Levon some years before, and how she must have been castigated by neighbors. He thought about her bed and her in her bed—so close but so far. He threw off the blanket.

It seemed like a long time had passed since he had told Martha of his plight. Keeping Tommy in or near the house, she had not talked to him or given any indication that she knew he was there. He saw this as possibly a good sign. If she was going to ask him to leave, she probably would have already done it. On the other hand, maybe she simply didn't want to talk to him at all. The uncertainty plagued Zach but he had to give her time.

31

Near Milledgeville, Georgia, 1864

ZACH AWOKE ABRUPTLY. He could hear one of the black men snoring, but everything else was quiet. The first light of day was a dim glow on the horizon. He sat up, wondering what was different, what was missing. He could see Jake staring at him across his manger, his ears at full alert, hoping it was time to be fed. Then he heard a soft rain on the roof, the barn amplifying the sound. He could smell the fresh moisture in the air as the breeze picked up.

It was the rooster. The rooster had not crowed his usual announcement of the new day.

Zach stood up, the waxed blanket crinkling, the hay yielding to his footfall with a soft crunch. Standing in the middle of the barn, he made a visual check of the inside. Everything seemed normal. His heart pounded in his chest, but he didn't know why.

Then he heard it. Just above the sound of the rain was the distant baying of a hound. Then another, and another. Zach walked to the door and looked toward the river. There was not enough light to see much, but he could see the outline of the trees that bordered the bank. The faint baying continued. He went back and woke Levon, who sat up alertly. Zach cupped his ears in the direction of the river and when Levon heard the dogs he jumped up, panic on his face. Zach held up his arms as if to shoot a rifle, asking Levon where the gun was. Levon pointed toward the house.

The two freed men awakened, and hearing the dogs, their eyes went wide with panic. They had heard bloodhounds before. Zach knew they were in deep trouble. He looked around the barn for a place to hide the men. Under a pile of hay would be the first place they would look. In the cellar would be the second. Zach crawled up the ladder to the mow and looked out the door toward the river. The baying of the hounds was distinct and moving up river toward them. He couldn't see them in the dim light, but he estimated them to be no more than a half mile away, which gave them ten minutes or less.

Zach told Levon to tell Martha to take Tommy and the rifle to the cellar and to shoot anybody that came down the steps without hesitation. He told Levon to stay with her and protect her no matter what. Meanwhile, he went to Jake's stall. Levon had piled Jake's manure in the back, planning for Zach to pitch it out when the pile got big enough. Zach motioned the two ex-slaves to come over. Both were shaking with fear, their faces turned upward as if seeking divine intervention. When they understood what Zach wanted, they said they did not want to cause trouble and they would just run for the river and float away. He thought about floating down the river with his metal breathing tube, but he knew it wouldn't work. They wouldn't be able to get to the river soon enough and it was much too shallow anyhow. Plus, he had only one tube.

He waved his hands, dismissing their idea, and motioned for them to crouch together in the back corner of Jake's stall. The two men were scared. Their faces contorted and beaded with sweat. Zach thought about the origin of their fear and it flashed through his mind that these men had probably had similar experiences before. While they huddled in the corner with their hands over their heads, Zach pitched Jake's manure over them, the ripe smell spreading throughout the barn. The pile had retained heat and let off steam as Zach pitched. Zach hoped the manure would mask the scent of the two ex-slaves.

Satisfied as he could be, Zach closed the back door of the barn and went out the large front doors, leaving them open. He saw Levon, Martha, and Tommy rushing toward the cellar. Just before she disappeared down the steps, she looked back at Zach. She, too, had panic on her face. Zach knew he would protect her at any cost. She hesitated, holding his gaze, then disappeared. Zach's heart soared.

Three hounds emerged from the trees and headed straight for the barn. The hounds put their noses to the ground then bayed and ran ahead for a few yards and did it all over again. As the dogs reached the midway point in the plowed field, three riders came into view. The horses' hooves sank into the plowed soil, leaving deep tracks. The riders peered through the rain toward the barn. All three men were hatless and without raincoats, their wet hair streaming down over their faces and shoulders, their rifle butts resting on their thighs at the ready. When they reached the middle of the field, they stopped.

The hounds reached the closed back door of the barn and immediately, their baying changed to long, mournful howls. Zach remembered that sound from his childhood when he hunted raccoons, the baying of a hound telling its master the prey was treed. Any hopes Zach may have had that the rain would wash the ex-slaves' scent away were dashed.

The three men appeared to be talking, deciding what to do. One laughed aloud, took a bottle out of his saddlebag, took a long pull, and passed it to another, who drank and passed it on. The bottle was passed around twice before one tipped it up empty and threw it in the field. Then they started toward the barn, their horses at a steady walk.

Zach stood in the rain on the other side of the barn, in front of the open doors, waiting for the men to approach. He felt the raindrops hitting his scalp through his already soaked hair, flowing down and dripping off his beard. He thought about what he would do if he had a rifle. He could easily shoot all three, but he wasn't convinced that shooting was going to be necessary.

As the men got close, he began to change his mind. He could see the men's eyes were wild, almost glazed over from drink. They sat heavy on their saddles, their heads not moving in unison with their horses' movements. Zach braced for the worst.

When they were within a hundred feet, they spread out and pulled their horses to a stop, facing him. "You got our niggers?" one asked.

Zach didn't know how to respond. He folded his arms across his chest and stared back at the riders.

"You got our niggers," the same man said, only this time it was not in the form of a question. The man wore a gray Confederate jacket, unbuttoned and hanging open, exposing a deep scar across his chest. Zach guessed he was not a soldier, and that he may have gotten the scar in a barroom brawl.

"I have two free black men here. They are not yours," Zach replied.

The same man spat, the thick brown fluid hitting a puddle with a plop. He lowered his rifle and pointed it directly at Zach. "We'll see about that. Zeb, go in there and git 'em. We know they're there." The hounds continued to howl.

The man named Zeb rode into the barn and dismounted, his legs unsteady.

Zach backed into the barn himself. "There is no property of yours in here," he said. "You'd best be riding on out of here. You're on private property."

"And what in the hell do you think you gonna do about it?" one said. "You gonna call the sheriff?" They laughed.

The one called Zeb was smaller than the other two and walked like a banty rooster, his bravado steeled by alcohol. He eyed the haymow, and with a knowing look, leaned his rifle against the wall, grabbed a pitchfork, and climbed up the ladder. He jammed the fork into the hay, each time in a different place, and each time laughing as if he expected to hit one of the ex-slaves. He eventually gave up, looking disappointed. "They ain't here," he said to the others, as if he'd just missed out on the last piece of cherry pie.

The other two rode into the barn, water dripping off them onto the dry red dirt floor. Jake brayed in his stall, his chin rising up, his long yellow teeth bared. Zeb turned around to start down the ladder, his foot searching for the first rung, the pitchfork still in hand.

The man with the gray coat looked around the barn. Then he saw the mound of manure behind Jake. "Zeb, go git 'em. They're under that pile of manure, sure as shit," he said, smiling at his own wit. "We'll hang 'em right here in the barn." He pulled a coiled rope out of his saddlebag.

When Zeb neared the bottom of the ladder, Zach grabbed the pitch-fork, easily wresting it away. Zeb stepped off the ladder, grabbed his rifle, and turned to face Zach. Zach knew he had little time. He thrust the fork at Zeb, the tines going deep into his belly. Zeb stared at the pitchfork in disbelief. His eyes were wide, his mouth contorted. He took several steps backward and fell to the ground with the pitchfork handle sticking gro-tesquely into the air. He screamed once, then lay silent, a gurgling sound coming from his throat.

Grey Coat spurred his horse closer to Zach and whipped the rifle barrel drunkenly at his head. Zach ducked, and the barrel grazed his forehead, cutting through the skin. Then Grey Coat put his rifle barrel right in front of Zach's face. "Looks like we gonna be hangin' three instead of two," he said. He dismounted and rammed the butt of his rifle into Zach's abdomen. Zach bent over in pain, gasped for breath, and slumped to the ground.

The hounds still howled outside. "Go shut those goddamned dogs up," Grey Coat said to the other. "We'll hang those two niggers and this guy." He kicked Zach in the ribs. "And then we'll git the hell outta here." The two ex-slaves knew they had been discovered and stood up, the manure matted in their hair and smeared on their clothes.

Grey Coat took two more lengths of rope out of his saddlebags and used two of them to tie the two Negroes' hands behind their backs. When he tried to tie Zach's hands, his body was too difficult to move, so he tied them in front of him.

The rain was falling harder now, making it difficult to hear inside the barn. The two worked quickly, one throwing two ropes over the main crossbeam, the other ordering the two ex-slaves to mount two of the horses. When they hesitated, he pulled the pitchfork out of Zeb. It made a sucking sound. He brandished it in front of them, blood dripping off the tines. They tightened two nooses to each of the ex-slave's necks and forced them to mount, then tied the other ends off tautly on a vertical support beam. With Zach still trying to catch his breath, they relaxed and one took out another bottle and both took long pulls at it, wiping their mouths and chins with their sleeves.

"Watch this. Now comes the good part," one said to Grey Coat, and he slapped the horses on their rumps. The two horses bolted, jerking the Negroes into the air with sickening, cracking sounds. The freedmen dangled, making rasping sounds, their feet and legs flailing the air. Grey Coat laughed, pointing to one whose neck was bent at almost a right angle, his mirth lighting up his face.

The dead men swung on the ends of their ropes, one bumping up against the other, which added to the murderers' glee.

"One more," one said to the other. He had noticed Zach was getting up. "This guy deserves to die for what he did to Zeb."

Zach was jerked to his feet. The pain in his gut was excruciating, but he could see the two black men dangling from the barn beam. He shook his head to clear his thoughts, blood dripping off his forehead. One of the men took a third noose and tied it around his neck. Grey Coat stood back with his rifle in hand, as the first man used the pitchfork to force Zach up on one of the horses. Zack felt the noose tighten as they tied the other end off on the same beam that held the two dead men.

His mind clear now, Zach thought about dying. He hoped Martha would stay in the cellar, and she and Levon would not be found.

"Do it," the man with the rifle said, and the other man slapped the horse forward. Zach's tied hands went up to the rope to relieve the pressure on his neck, and as he came completely out of the saddle, his hands absorbed the shock of the rope. He pulled on the noose to give himself air. The rough hemp dug into his neck. The harder he pulled, the tighter it became. He began to black out.

Then a rifle shot. Blood splattering all around. The man who had slapped the horse fell to the ground, the back of his head a bloody void. Zach felt himself hit the ground, his knees buckling. He saw that Levon was there and that he had cut the rope. Then he saw Martha standing in the doorway, the rifle still pressed to her shoulder, rain and tears dripping off her face.

Frantic, Levon waved his hands, looking at Grey Coat. Grey Coat pointed his rifle at Martha.

"No!" Zach leapt at the man. He saw the man's finger tighten on the trigger. The gun discharged just as Zach hit him. Zach took the man's head in both hands, and in a rage, smashed it against a peg in a barn beam. The peg penetrated the man's skull, and when Zach released his grip, the man hung from the peg, his body twitching.

With a deep breath, he turned around and saw Levon running to Martha. She was on the ground. Zach was there instantly, cradling her head on his knee. Rain beaded on her forehead. She wore an almost placid smile. Then he saw the round red mark just below her ribcage, and his heart sank. He saw blood flowing from underneath her, mixing with surface water, puddling in his shoe imprints, frothy pink.

She opened her eyes and reached up to him. He leaned closer, looking into her eyes. She whispered, "Please take care of Tommy." Then her finger went to his face and traced his scar. Her eyes glazed and her hand fell to her side. Blood dripped from Zach's forehead, merging with hers in the turgid, red Georgia mud.

32

Knoxville, Tennessee, 1908

CHRIS WALKED BACK to the Lamar Hotel and went directly to his room. When Zach had finished his story, he had tried not to show his emotions, but he had violated one of his own rules: do not get emotionally involved in any story. He sat at the little table and tried to finish the story to send back to New York. The image of Martha's last seconds was clear in his mind, and he wept. While he knew Zach's story was not typical, he realized all soldiers surely had tragic war experiences that would haunt them for the rest of their lives.

———

"Sure hope you come back and see us sometime soon," Jerome said, as Chris checked out the next morning.

"Knoxville is my kind of place," Chris said. "My job is done here, but I've grown to love this town and its people."

"Catching the noon train to Pittsburg?" Jerome asked, sliding Chris's bill over for approval.

"Yep. I'll stop at Western Union, then the train station." He paid the bill and handed some coins to Jerome. "Thanks for your help. I have a new appreciation for Jack Daniels."

As Chris turned to go, Jerome said, "Almost forgot. Mr. Harkin told me to give this to you." He handed Chris an envelope.

"Hmm. Was he here already this morning?"

"Came in at six. He was all smiles. Asked me if I wanted to have supper with him tonight."

Chris put the envelope in his case, then headed to the Western Union office. The sky was clear and the air was brisk. He heard the familiar sound of shod horses on the brick street. *Nothing like New York City,* he thought. After wiring his report to his editor, Chris stood outside the Western Union office and took a deep breath. He felt relieved that Zach's final chapter had been sent. He had changed nothing, and he knew Pulitzer would be irate. He pictured him leaning back in his chair with his face getting redder and redder.

Then Chris thought about Sarah. She wouldn't like the report either. Nothing would ever change her mind about Sherman.

He had a few hours before his train left, and on a whim, he decided to pay his respects to John Hearn, the editor of the *Knoxville Sentinel.*

A bell tinkled as Chris entered. Behind a desk sat a man with a green bill pulled over his eyes. As nobody else was in the room, Chris asked if he could see Mr. Hearn.

"If you're not blind, you are seeing him now," the man said, standing, the wheels on his wooden chair were in need of oil. The man was tall, heavy set, with a stern face that looked to Chris like he rarely smiled. He did not offer his hand. Without saying so, he appeared to be asking what Chris wanted.

"I'm Chris Martin, from *The New York World,* and I just thought I would drop in and say hello. I've been in your town on and off for the…"

"Martin. You're the reporter on the Harkin story," Hearn interrupted. "I've been hearing about your articles from some of my New York friends. Nice work. Somebody finally got Harkin to talk. Have a seat. Coffee?"

Chris took the chair indicated, which was exactly like Hearn's. It protested loudly as Chris sat. "Thank you, sir," Chris said. "I'm catching the noon train to Pittsburg. I think my work here is finished."

An older woman came in the back door, carrying a mug of coffee. The mug had several chips in it and appeared none too clean, but the coffee was strong and hot. The woman disappeared back the way she had come, and

Hearn lit up a cigar. Hearn asked how Chris had gotten Harkin to talk and indicated he had tried several times.

"Sure had nothing to do with my powers of persuasion," Chris said. "I think Zach just thought it might help him to get it off his chest. I happened to be in the right place at the right time."

"From what I hear, the whole City of New York is in love with your story. I heard Pulitzer is selling more papers than ever," Hearn said.

"Pulitzer prints what people want to hear. Sometimes I think he would prefer to bend the truth a bit to increase circulation. We're at an impasse over Colonel Wirz, from Andersonville," Chris said.

Chris looked around the office. The furniture was tattered, but comfortable. Hearn's desk was a roll top and so stacked with papers and books that rolling down the top would have been impossible. He could hear the stomp-stomp of the press in the back. The smell of ink hung heavy in the air. He liked it.

Hearn seemed surprised that Pulitzer was directly involved, bypassing the editor. He said he was frequently tempted to spice stories up to gain readership, but he believed in solid, robust, and honest journalism. Chris felt at ease with Hearn.

Before Chris realized it, he had to leave to catch the train. He shook Hearn's hand, and Hearn said, "I'm seventy years old, Chris. I sure could use somebody like you around here. I miss people with good journalistic instincts. Lord knows, we don't have any in Tennessee."

33

New York City, New York, 1908

THREE DAYS LATER, Chris was not surprised when he couldn't spot Sarah in the throng of people waiting at the ferry. His train had been delayed, and he'd missed his connection in Pittsburg. He decided to walk uptown for a while, to get his blood circulating again. The darkening sky was cloudy, but the temperature was mild. He passed a newsstand and picked up the evening edition of *The World*. Sitting on a park bench under a streetlight, he leafed through the paper, looking for his story. The story had usually been printed on the inside front cover, but as he scanned each page, his heart sank. He found it at last on the back page.

In large, bold print across the top, the headline read, *The Scars of War: Zach Harkin, by Chris Martin*. A young man sat down on the bench next to him. He seemed to have been looking for suitable light, as he had *The World* folded over to Zach's article. The young man sat on the edge of the bench, holding the paper close to his eyes, his head moving back and forth as he read each line.

He looked over at Chris, and seemed to realize for the first time that they were both reading the same article. "Can you believe this horseshit?" the young man said, his face contorted into a sneer. "Sherman should have burned the whole state of Georgia. Top to bottom. Burned everything. He just didn't have the balls."

Chris didn't know if he should engage the man not, but finally he asked, "Why?"

The man looked at Chris. "You kidding?" Then, when he saw that Chris was serious, he said, "Because they enslaved all those poor black folks, that's why." His voice was incredulous.

Chris thought about this young man whose emotions were so strong. Forty plus years, and nothing had changed. He did not respond, but tried to finish the article in the fading light. Not hearing an answer, the young man rolled up the paper, slammed it down on the bench, and left.

———

"Sarah, I'm home," Chris yelled as he came through the front door. Lost in thought, he had ended up walking all the way to his apartment. The place was dark.

He lit a lamp and went to the bedroom. "Sarah?" He turned around and walked back to the entrance hall and took off his coat. On the table, where he always put his keys, was an envelope. His name was written on the front in Sarah's handwriting.

He took the envelope into the living room, poured himself a strong drink, and sat in his favorite chair. After staring at his name for several minutes, he opened it. The terse message read: *Chris, I've decided to go back to Milledgeville for a while. Love, S.*

Chris got up and made himself another drink. Then, another.

———

"Top floor, please," Chris told the elevator man. The door closed, and the car rumbled upward, bouncing gently side to side.

"The big man in this morning?" Chris asked.

"Every day, seven days a week," the man replied.

The door slid open, and Chris entered the office. "Mr. Pulitzer?" Chris asked.

"Go right in," the receptionist said. "He's been looking for you. The door's open."

The window behind Pulitzer's desk was opaque with clouds. Pulitzer sat in his chair with his back to the door. "Mr. Pulitzer?" Chris said.

"Martin. Sit down," Pulitzer said, slowly rotating his chair to face him. He didn't get up, and issued no greeting. "You read the paper?"

"Yes, sir. Looked good."

"That may be, but evidently we are still not understanding each other, and I find that unacceptable."

Chris stayed standing. "I think we have understood each other from the beginning," he said. "I think the problem is that we do not agree."

"Martin, I told you what I wanted you to say. I told you I wanted you to make some changes. You didn't. That, Martin, is not just a 'misunderstanding,' it's insubordination."

Chris could feel the anger in Pulitzer's voice, but to him, it was uncalled for. He took off his glasses and held them up to the light, then pulled out a handkerchief and started to clean the lenses, even though they weren't dirty.

"Insubordination is a strong word, sir. I believe it means 'disobedience,' and if you order me to commit malfeasance, then I have every right to be disobedient."

Pulitzer's eyes narrowed. He stared at Chris is face slowly reddening as the meaning of what he'd said sank in.

"I have another opportunity, Mister Pulitzer. So, with all due respect, I've written my last story for *The World*." Chris took a step toward the door.

Pulitzer's veins stood out in his neck. He looked up at Chris, his mouth open as if to say something. Chris walked out and closed the door behind him. The receptionist looked at him with a twinkle in her eye. "Nobody has ever said anything like that to Mr. Pulitzer," she whispered.

Leaving the *World* building, Chris felt relieved. He realized he was hungry, so he stopped in at P.J. Clarke's for a good hamburger. Clarke's was a hangout for other journalists, and he knew he could also get a stiff drink. He sat at a corner table, and several other newsmen stopped to shake his hand on the series about Zach Harkin. While the accolades made him feel good, he also realized that probably not many of them would have done what he had just done. He had been on top, working for the biggest newspaper in the country, and had just captivated the city with his story. He didn't tell any of them he was now unemployed.

Several hours later, he left the restaurant and headed back to his apartment. He passed the Western Union office on the way, and stopped. He entered, took a telegram form, and wrote the following message: *Mr. Hearn. Will arrive your office next week to assume my new duties with the Knoxville Sentinel.*

Back at his apartment, Chris decided to write Sarah a letter to let her know about his new job. He couldn't find a pencil, and when he opened his case, he saw the envelope Jerome had given him.

He sat down and opened it and read.

Dear Mr. Martin,

As you know, when you first contacted me to talk about the war for your paper, I was quite hesitant. To be truthful, I did not want to go through the pain of remembering. However, as time went on, and with your patience, I became more at ease in telling my story.

After you left last night, I had dinner alone as usual and then went to bed. And for the first time in many, many years, I fell right to sleep. I slept soundly. However, something woke me up in the middle of the night. I lit my lamp, and there he was, sitting on the end of my bed again, the dead sharpshooter, Jack Kavandish. Only this time, his jaw wasn't missing. His black beard was as I remembered it when I looked through the scope of my gun over forty years ago. He looked me in the eye, stood, and walked toward the door. He stopped and continued to stare at me a moment. His eyes didn't have that wild, angry look anymore. Rather, they were soft. Maybe even kind. He nodded, ever so slightly, and left the room, closing the door behind him.

Today, the sun is shining again. Thank you.

Your friend,

Zach

THE END

HOME AGAIN
A Civil War Novel

Exclusive Bonus Excerpt

On Sale Now

For more on upcoming events and media, visit
www.michaelkennethsmith.com

Follow me on Twitter
Like me on Facebook
Join me on Pinterest
Shelve me on Goodreads

Eastern Tennessee, September 1859

A LARGE SYCAMORE TREE projected out of a riverbank ten feet above the water's edge. Zach and his father were perched on the outcropping, Zach fishing downstream and his dad fishing upstream. Between them, leaning against the tree, was a loaded Enfield musket and a can of worms.

Zach's father glanced back up the bank behind them. "Son, we have a big copperhead crawling down over the top of the bank right toward us. Do you want him?"

Zach looked back quickly, picked up the gun, cocked the hammer, turned, instinctively aimed the rifle and fired before the stock reached his shoulder. The sound reverberated down the river valley and the headless snake fell down the bank and hit Zach's father in the back, writhing violently. In his death throes, the large snake wrapped his body around Zach's father's waist, tightening its grip. The snake was trying to bite him reflexively, even though he had no means of doing so.

"Don't know why he's so mad at you," Zach said. "You didn't do anything to him."

"You are faster with that rifle than most are with a pistol," his father said laughing.

"Just doing what you taught me, Dad," Zach said as he pitched the snake into the water.

"Say, we're about out of worms, so I'll walk over to that barnyard we passed a while ago and look for some more. You stay here and fish. We need a few more to have a nice mess to eat tonight."

Zach was fourteen years old. Every September, he and his father took a week to float a river in eastern Tennessee to fish, hunt a little and live off the land. It always marked the end of the summer and it was the highlight. When Zach was two, his father and mother moved from England to Manchester, Vermont, where his father set up a small gun shop. However, the community turned out to be too small to support the business, so they moved to Knoxville, Tennessee, where the business thrived. This year, they had decided to go down the Obed River, which was a little west of Knoxville, near the small town of Crossville.

Zach was adding a nice bullhead to the stringer of fish when he heard the hoot of an owl. Then he heard the neigh of a horse and immediately looked up, scanning the woods behind him. He grabbed the musket and went up the bank looking for the horse. He was very comfortable in the woods by himself because most summers he hunted every day. Just as he saw the swish of a sorrel's tail in front of him, he felt the cold steel of a rifle in the middle of his back.

"You are trespassing on private property," a boyish voice said. "And you are fishing in my private hole. Who are you?"

Zach was shocked that anybody could sneak up on him like that without a sound. He turned around and saw a thin freckle-faced boy with an old flintlock rifle aimed menacingly at him.

"Zach Harkin. We're just floating down the river like we do every year at this time. We didn't know this was your private fishing hole."

"Who's 'we'?" said the boy.

"My father and I. He went looking for more worms just over yonder."

The boy slowly lowered his rifle. "You fishing with worms?"

"Yes, and we've caught quite a few."

"You mean those little things on that stringer there?"

Zach picked up the mocking tone of the boy's voice. "You know a better way?"

"Sure do. Grubs."

"Grubs? Never heard of that. Where do you find them?"

"Keep a whole box of them in the ground just above where you where fishing." The boy studied Zach's face for a moment. "Want to try them?"

"Sure. We just need a couple more for tonight's supper."

"Looking at the size of those you have caught, you could catch a dozen more and you would still starve to death." The boy gave out a hoot owl whistle and the sorrel horse neighed and came right over to where they were standing. "Say hello to Bonnie."

Zach realized he had been outsmarted. When he had heard the first owl call, his attention had been drawn by the neigh of the horse, which allowed the boy to sneak up on him from behind. He was impressed. Together they walked back to the bank just above the sycamore tree. The boy kicked the dirt, exposing a wooden lid to a buried box. He reached in and pulled a handful of grubs. "Here try one of these," he said. "Hook it from the tail to its head. Then cast the grub down on the riverbank and let the grub bounce into the water."

Zach crawled down to the tree outcropping and after hooking the grub as the boy asked, flung the bait on the bank and watched it tumble into the water.

"Get ready," the boy said.

Seconds later the line went taut, the pole dipped down and Zach had to hang on. The line swished through the water as the fish tried to get away. Zach feared the line would break and pulled as hard as he dared until the fish finally came to the surface. The boy scrambled down to the water's edge and expertly grabbed the large black bass by the gills and hoisted it into the air. It weighed at least six or seven pounds.

"Now you have some real supper," the boy said.

The bass was bigger than all the rest of the fish put together. The boy proudly stuck out his hand. "I'm Luke Pettigrew," he said. "That's the way we do things around here."

"Well, I'll be..."

Just then Zach's father came up and stared at the bass. "Guess we have a lot to learn about fishing in this river."

Zach jumped in. "Dad, this is Luke. He lives around here. I, er, we caught this thing with a grub."

"Nice to meet you, Luke."

"He has a whole box of grubs in this box here," Zach said.

Zach's father said, "Its getting late in the day. Care to join us for supper? Our camp is just upstream a little ways. Will your folks mind?"

"Nope. My father lets me go out all the time; he won't care. Whenever I get home, it'll be alright with him."

"Okay, let's get cracking," Zach's father said as he led the way back to the camp.

It was dark by the time Zach dropped the large fillets into the sizzling frying pan. The fish had been cleaned and scaled and Luke had found some wild onions.

"You ever do any coon hunting?" Luke asked Zach.

"Not so much over our way. We pretty much stick to other animals like groundhogs, rabbits and squirrels. Besides, don't you need dogs for coons?"

"Yes, I got a real nice coon dog named Jeff. We like to start out just after it gets good and dark. We walk through the woods and when ole Jeff picks up a scent, off he goes. Some coon hunters like to wait for their dogs to tree the coon, then they ride their horses over to the tree. Me, I like to run with the dog, stay right with him. More fun that way."

"Now that does sound like fun. Ever try a groundhog from five hundred yards?" Zach countered. "I like to go out just before it gets light in the morning and wait for 'em to come out of their dens."

"Five hundred yards? Wow. You must have a special rifle for that. That musket you have won't go that far, will it?"

"No, it won't, but dad's a gunsmith and he has a couple of rifles that are accurate well beyond five hundred yards."

"Hmmm. I could sit on my back porch and shoot squirrels without even putting my shoes on."

The sweet aroma of the fish frying wafted through the campsite as all three dug in. Halfway through the supper, the sound of an approaching horse interrupted their enjoyment. Luke immediately jumped up as if he knew what was happening.

A man on a large chestnut rode right into the camp. "Luke, where in the hell have you been?" the man said, "You know you are expected to be home before milking time. I had to get the cows in myself. You are the most irresponsible boy the world. Get home. Now."

Luke got up promptly and left without a word. He did a back flip onto his horse and rode away.

"Who in the hell do you think you are?" the man said to Zach and his father. "You are on private property and you better not be here when I get up in the morning." He kicked his horse and disappeared in the night.

2

Zach

March 1862

THE SUN HAD just illuminated the far hillside. The spider lines of Zach's rifle followed the two young groundhogs as they climbed from the hole of their den to the top of the hill. The sun's rays had melted most of the snow over the last several days. Lying on the ground, using an old butternut log to steady his rifle, Zach felt the cold dampness of the early spring earth through his long wool underwear. The groundhogs' fur shimmered. They were both healthy and had eaten plenty of corn in the surrounding fields. The distance was about nine hundred yards, and with a muzzle velocity of twelve hundred feet per second, Zach quickly – intuitively – calculated his bullet would take almost two and one half seconds to reach the target. He knew as soon as the first hog was hit, the second would instantly make for his den. Groundhogs could move at lightning speed. His scope was sighted in at five hundred yards; he needed another two feet of elevation to hit his prey. He felt a slight breeze from the left and he moved the scope's cobweb spider lines slightly to correct. As the second hog rose to survey the surroundings, Zach tried to control his breathing as he always did on long-distance shots, being careful not to fog the lens of the scope. The smell of the thawing earth rose to his nostrils, mixing with the fumes of the gun oil he had applied the night before. Pressing his cheek to the custom-made walnut gunstock, he felt the silky coolness of the wood. His right hand tightened on the rifle grip. It, too, had been custom-made to fit his hand. The bill of his hunting cap shielded his eyes and helped him focus on the target. He relaxed his arm and shoulders to be able to hold the spider lines without movement. He rubbed his trigger finger on the side of the gunstock to increase sensitivity. Finger on the trigger now, he went through his normal ritual... deep breath in... exhale... half-breath in... hold. Steady now, he squeezed the hair trigger and the modified Spencer sent a 52-caliber bullet on its way to his prey more than half a mile away. Before the bullet arrived, Zach, with practiced lightning speed, ejected the shell and pumped a new one into the chamber. Anticipating the second groundhog would high-tail it to its den, he moved the spider lines to the mouth of the den fifteen feet below. Compensating for the wind and elevation and before the second hog appeared in his scope, Zach squeezed the trigger again. The smoke from the two shots slowly drifted off and the pungent odor of the black powder perme-ated the air. He held the spider lines on that spot while he waited the two and one half seconds for the bullet to travel the half-mile. Sure enough, the second groundhog arrived at the hole the exact same instant the bullet arrived. Both groundhogs lay motionless as the echoes of the two gunshots reverberated down the valley once, and then again. Zach broke into a wide grin.

Sitting behind Zach were his father, Tom Harkin, and Jim Luttrell. Both had arrived with Zach some thirty minutes before. Luttrell was the mayor of Knoxville and reputed to be a fine marksman himself. They had seen the whole event with spyglasses that were twice as powerful as the rifle-mounted Davidson 4X scope Zach had used.

Visibly impressed Luttrell said, "Let me see that gun, son." He rubbed his hand over the fine finish. "Damn, Tom, you are good."

"Takes more than just a good rifle to hit a target like that, though, Jim. Zach, go get them; we'll wait here," Tom said.

Zach, still smiling, got up. Standing his full six feet, he wiped the dirt off his front and took off his cap. His long dark hair fell down over his brown eyes, and he immediately brushed it back. "I can smell it now...roasted groundhog stuffed with apple, yummmm...I'll be right back." He took off to pick up the dead quarry. He would skin the groundhogs, and his mother would roast them as only his mother could do.

Luttrell turned to Tom. "Quite a boy you have there."

"We are proud of him. Pity any animal he's hunting; they don't have a chance."

"Tom, he'd sure make a good soldier. You going to let him sign up?"

"He sure wants to, but Lizzie and I are dragging our feet."

"He'd make a great sharpshooter."

"But how could we manage that?"

"Got an idea, Tom. Let me work on it. Think you could hold Zach off for a couple of weeks?"

Several moments later, Zach returned with the groundhogs. Both were nice and fat, about ten to twelve pounds. He took out his hunting knife and quickly skinned and cleaned the animals. He used a unique style he had developed over the years that kept him from getting his hands dirty. After depositing them in a gunnysack, Zach joined the two men on the walk back, about a mile away.

Tom Harkin, a noted gunsmith from Manchester, England, arrived in Vermont with his wife, Lizzie, and his only son in 1857. He had worked at the Whitworth Rifle Company as a design engineer. He loved to work on guns, always trying to improve them, to make them shoot faster, straighter and farther. An independent and adventurous man, he tired of working for a large company and decided to move to America, where he'd been told he'd find great opportunities. He initially chose Manchester, in Vermont, because he reasoned it must have been settled by people from his own Manchester, and the transition would be easier for Lizzie and Zach.

Tom built a small workshop in the family's new three-room log home and hung out a shingle. Their house was right next to the Charles Orvis home, and to Orvis' tackle shop, and Tom thought business would be good next to each other. But the village of Manchester turned out to be too small to sustain enough business, so after working hard for almost a year, the Harkins decided to move to Knoxville, Tennessee. They purchased a small house near the corner of Gay and Union Streets and set out a shingle again. The gunsmith commerce was small but steady, and provided a modest income for the family. The scope mount Tom had devised attracted a fair amount of interest. The original Whitmore design had the scope side-mounted, with the rear portion located near the shooter's eye. While quite effective, this caused a lot of eye bruising from the recoil of the rifle. Tom's solution was to mount the scope on top of the rifle and slightly forward, allowing the shooter a clearer field of vision and greatly reducing the recoil effect on the eyes. The disadvantage of the top mount was it rendered the conventional open sights on the barrel useless. The shooter did not have the choice of the open sight or the scope. Only the scope could be used with the top mount. As a result, when the target was identified with the naked eye, the time needed to sight in and fire was longer.

Harkin also modified the way the bullets were fed into the firing chamber. Ideally a Sharps rifle would be better suited for long-range shooting, however, he liked the Spencer's unique design for more rapid firing. The Sharps was a muzzleloader that required a lengthy procedure to load, limiting the shooter to two to four shots per minute, depending on the shooter's experience. The Spencer, while much lighter, had a hole in the stock from the shoulder butt plate through to the chamber in which the bullets could be stored and held ready for rapid shooting. It was possible to extract a casing and insert another so fast that an experienced user could fire shots every three seconds or less.

The Spencer rifle Zach used had this top-mounted scope. Tom had also installed a longer barrel and forestock to allow for improved long-range accuracy. Also, the barrel was rifled to spin the bullet faster than either the Sharps or the factory-made Spencer. This design change was tested over and over again and proved to be another measurable improvement. Lastly, he added more black powder to the rimfire cartridges, substantially increasing the penetrating power and range. With the mounted scope, the longer, heavier barrel, and increased cartridge power, the gun was limited to prone- or sitting-position shooting. It was a gun ideally suited for fast, long-range shooting. It was a gun ideally suited for a sharpshooter.

That night, the aroma of roasting groundhog permeated the small house as Lizzie Harkin busied herself preparing dinner for Tom and Zach. She was born Elizabeth Medford in Manchester, England, on this exact date forty years ago. Lizzie and Tom were childhood sweethearts. She lived four houses down the street from the Harkin family home and had been attracted to Tom because of his somewhat shy demeanor and independent streak. Lizzie was diminutive in stature and Tom, being slightly over six feet, proved sometimes opposites do attract. She had mid-length auburn hair, dark blue eyes and a beautiful fair complexion. From a very early age, she knew Tom Harkin was going to be the man of her life, and although the job was not too difficult, she made sure he felt the same way. They were married in October 1844. On July 10th, 1845, their only son, Zachary, was born. Complications during childbirth prevented them from having more children, and Zach became the center of their lives.

"When do we eat?" yelled Zach as he sauntered into the kitchen area. "If I don't eat soon I'll shrivel up and die from lack of food." He grinned and hugged his mother.

"As soon as you wash your hands, set the table and pour some water, we will be ready," said Lizzie. "And you might want to call your father and have him wash up, also."

After they were seated around the table, Tom raised his water in a toast and said, "Lizzie, here's to your next forty years." Birthdays were not celebrated in the Harkin house, and Lizzie flushed. She was not surprised Tom remembered. He always remembered.

During the meal, the conversation was stilted. The war weighed heavily on their minds, but no one said anything. Finally, Zach managed to say, "Father?" He desperately wanted his parent's – particularly his father's – permission to sign up.

Tom took a deep breath. "Son, your mother and I dearly do not want you to go off to this senseless war. We do not believe in this war. If some of the Southern states want to secede from the Union, why should we sacrifice so much to keep them in. Some would say they have a clear right to secede anytime they want to."

"I could forbid you to go," Tom continued. "However, you just might run out there and sign up anyway. You would end up serving under some city-bred officer who wouldn't know beans about war and tactics. Jim has a couple ideas and promised to get back in a couple weeks. Then you can decide."

On a rainy afternoon a several weeks later, Jim Luttrell strode into Tom's little shop.

"Hello, Tom. Have any hot coffee? I'm soaked."

Lizzie always kept a pot of coffee on the stove so customers could sit and relax while they talked about guns. Everybody loved to talk guns, and everybody wanted to talk to Tom about guns because he was the recognized resident expert.

Tom poured a mug for Jim and another for himself.

Jim started. "Tom, as our mayor, I have become a friend of John Sherman, who was a U.S. congressman and now has been elected to the Senate, representing the state of Ohio. I have exchanged telegrams with him about Zach and where he might go in the service to best utilize his unique skills, while keeping in mind your and Lizzie's deep concern for his safety." John sipped some of the hot coffee and continued, "Sherman's brother is an officer in the Western Army and..."

"You don't mean William Tecumseh Sherman, do you, Jim?"

"The same," John said.

"But I thought he was being treated for insanity. Didn't I read a short while ago he was sent back East for treatment?"

"Quite right," said Jim. "However, doctors quickly determined he was perfectly sound. He has some nervous twitches and a lot of nervous energy, but General Grant thinks he is an up-and-comer. The word is, he is a level-headed general when he is under fire. His twitches go away and he is extremely competent.

"Furthermore, he wrote to his brother not long ago indicating his need for young men with Zach's talents. Tom, I think if Zach would travel down to Fort Donelson or wherever Sherman might be, the general would make him a sharpshooter. That would mean he would not necessarily be in the front lines of this fighting. He would be one half-mile in the rear of the front lines, maybe behind a log, picking his targets one by one."

Tom weighed what his friend had just said. His son was going to war one way or the other, and this idea seemed to greatly increase Zach's chances of survival. On the other hand, he would be so far from home, probably over five hundred miles from home...

"Jim, I don't like it, but it does offer some distinct advantages."

"Sure it does, Tom, and it appears this Western front is going very well. Our men out there might just be able to stop the South from adequately supplying their armies. Why Zach will be home before the end of the year, ready to join you in your business. Next year at this time, he will have found a wife and you'll be getting ready to become a grandfather."

"Okay, okay. Before you have me in the grave, we'll talk it over with Zach. Sure appreciate your help. Lizzie is worried to death."

That evening at the supper table, Zach could tell his father had something to say. Whenever he did, he would be very quiet – as if he were trying to search for the right words and for the right time to say them. He was very quiet tonight.

"Was Mr. Luttrell here today, Father?" Zach asked.

"Yes, and that is what your mother and I want to talk to you about, Zach."

Tom described the arrangements Luttrell had made.

"You mean I'm going out West? As part of Grant's army? As a sharp-shooter? Hoorah!!!! When can I go?"

"Just as soon as a letter of passage comes from General Sherman. But I think there is something very important you need to understand." Tom sat back in his chair, glanced at Lizzie and continued, "Zach, you were born with a gun in your hand. You were shooting rabbits before you knew how to spell your name. You shoot birds, squirrels, groundhogs, fox, deer, anything that moves, and you are good at it, better than I ever was. But let me tell you something, Zach. When you put those spider lines on a man, a human being, you will feel differently. A human being is not a groundhog, not a squirrel hiding in a tree. Someday you will have your sights on an enemy soldier, and you will have the power to end that person's life. That enemy soldier will be another human just like you are, with parents at home, maybe a girlfriend or wife. And you, by merely pulling the trigger, will be able to end that life." Tom waited to let Zach absorb what he had just said and then continued, "When you realize what that means, what that really means, you may think differently."

"I understand, Father, but maybe it will be shoot or get shot. I think I will do what I have to do to help quell this rebellion, and if that means taking another's life, I will do it."

Tom stood up from the table, indicating the meal was over. "You might be right, Zach, then again, you might be wrong. Whatever the case, your mother and I still don't want you to go but…"

"I know, Father, but I'll probably only be gone for a couple of months."

"You write us often," his mother said softly as she put her hand on Zach's.

3

Luke

March 1862

LUKE COULD FEEL the rhythm of the big mare as she galloped full speed down the rain-soaked cow path. As usual, he rode without saddle or bridle, guiding the horse with his feet and body. He urged her, "C'mon big girl, we gotta round up the cows before Pa figures out we've been lollygagging!"

Just as they rounded a slight bend, Luke saw a stream ahead. The heavy rain had swollen the normally three-foot-wide creek to over twenty feet. Luke leaned back, pulling the mare's mane slightly to slow a bit. The horse eyed the swollen stream and Luke could feel her hesitate. With a gentle nudge and a reassuring pat, he urged her on. Luke leaned well forward and she leaped to the other side, rider and horse seemingly as one.

Clearing the stream, Luke tapped the mare's neck on the left side to leave the path and head into the woods. He knew where the three cows were likely to go when it rained. Cutting through the woods would save a couple of minutes. The trees were thick and Luke let the sorrel mare thread her own way forward. She approached a low-hanging limb, and Luke had to slide down to the side of the horse. Hooking his right foot over the mare's back and wrapping his arms around her neck, he gasped. "Gal dang it, when are you going to learn to give me a little more room?" Just as they got past the obstacle,

Luke had to quickly right himself to avoid being walloped by another tree ahead.

Luke wasn't sure, but he suspected the horse had done it on purpose. She was always cranky when heading away from the barn. He thought the horse might be a little smarter than he gave her credit. Turn her back toward the barn, and she always gave him more room; she seemed to have reserve speed only when returning home.

Finally they cleared the woods. Sure enough, the three cows were in a small meadow, munching on wild clover. When Luke appeared, they immediately lined up head-to-tail down the cow path and began moving toward the barn, about a mile's walk away. Luke jumped off briefly to relieve himself and give his horse a breather. After several minutes, he remounted using his own peculiar, well-practiced method.

When Luke was about ten years old, his parents took him to a circus that was touring through eastern Tennessee. The circus had a trick rider who, when mounting a horse, stood on the right side facing forward, grabbed the mane with his left hand and somersaulted backwards, landing on the horse's back, facing forward. It was the cleverest thing Luke had ever seen. Back home, he tried to do it, without success. Luke needed time to grow and strengthen his stomach muscles. He did sit-ups, as many as two hundred a day, every day. He learned quickly to do a back flip, but never got up high enough to reach the horse's back. As he got older, he used a milking stool to give him the height he needed. Eventually, when he was about thirteen, he was able to do it without a stool. From then on, it was the way he preferred to mount a horse.

When the cows reached the overflowing stream, they needed a nudge to go into the water. It was not deep, and they waded across without difficulty. Suddenly, Luke saw movement in some low bushes. He pulled up short and waited for whatever was moving to show itself. After several moments, a red fox wove its way into view and Luke's heart started pounding with excitement.

He quickly calculated the cows would get to the barn without any further prompting — it was not far away. In a split second, Luke decided to chase.

He tapped his heels on the mare's haunches, leaned forward and slapped the left side of her neck. She responded instantly. In three powerful strides, she was at full gallop. The fox, hearing the sound of the hooves, quickly turned to run as it saw the large animal bearing down. The race was on.

Luke had no idea what he would do if he caught up with the fox. He had chased foxes before and all he knew was he loved the chase. He loved riding at breakneck speed — turning, swerving, jumping — doing whatever was necessary to stay close to the fox. He was addicted to the feeling he had when he communicated with his horse using only his body. The horse turned right when he leaned right. She would slow up when he leaned back, speed up as he leaned forward.

They zigged, then zagged. They made large circular turns left and right. The fox was wily and fast. Luke knew where the fox's den was, and the fox was moving in that direction. Up ahead was a large briar patch. The fox slipped into it. Luke figured it would exit the briars in the direction of the den, so he veered the mare to the right, toward the far end of the patch. Sure enough, the fox exited the briars just before Luke got there and the chase continued.

Luke could sense the horse tiring. The fox went under a fallen tree. Just as the mare jumped over, the fox made a hard right. Luke leaned hard right and the horse responded. The grass was long and wet from the rain. The mare turned so sharply her hooves slid out from under her and she went down. Luke had felt her slipping, anticipated the fall, and raised his right leg to avoid getting it smashed under her body. Both were down. The horse frantically tried to get up, pawing the ground with her hooves to gain traction to right herself. She managed to get all four legs under her and stood without moving. She did not put any weight on her right rear leg.

Luke, having been tossed clear, also rose unsteadily. With a sinking feeling, he approached the horse. She had fear in her eyes. As he embraced her head, she calmed a bit. He ran his hands down her right side to assess the damage. Everything appeared normal, with no obvious broken bones. However, she was very reluctant to put any weight on her back right leg. He massaged the area for some time and eventually she was able to hobble forward. They started back toward the barn very slowly. Then he started to think about his

SCARRED

father and how mad he would be when he found out about the mare's injury. They had only two horses, an older draft horse and the sorrel. The draft was used to haul the wagon around the small farm and occasionally to take the buggy to town to get supplies. The sorrel was needed for many daily chores.

Their progress was tedious and Luke could tell the mare was in pain. With each hobbling step she sounded a low, guttural groan. When they finally got back to the barn, he was greeted by a red-faced, very angry father. It was ten in the morning and Luke was late by about two hours.

Luke felt very little attachment to the horse. They had named her "Bonnie," but he did not consider her a pet. Farm animals — horses, cows — were an integral part of a farm's operation, much like a buggy or a plow. They were one of the tools a farmer had at his disposal to do his work. The animals were cared for and fed, but they were expected to work and earn their keep. If an animal could not perform those duties, then that animal was a drain on the homestead.

Luke's father took one look at the hobbled horse and another at Luke, who was bruised and scratched. His face turned even redder, "What the hell have you done this time? Do you have any idea how much we need that horse?" His raised his voice louder and louder. "How in the Sam Hill can I run this farm with this kind of behavior? When are you ever going to grow up, boy?" He pointed his finger at Luke, his hand shaking, his eyes looking big—ready to pop out. "Get your sorry ass over to the woodshed. Now."

Luke walked slowly toward the woodshed. He knew he was in deep trouble. He had never seen his father so angry. To make matters worse, the cows must not have made it back to the barn as he had hoped. And he knew his riding after the fox had been foolhardy and immature. He had put the horse at risk when it was not necessary.

Luke's father was a hard man who had lived a difficult life. In the summer of 1840, Jonas Lucas Pettigrew arrived in Crossville, Tennessee, a very small town near the western slopes of the Appalachian Mountains on the Cumberland Plateau. He was driving a team of draft horses that were pulling a small covered wagon in which he had placed all of his worldly belongings. He had previously worked on various farms and had saved his money, and now he meant to acquire some land and farm for himself. Jonas had lost his beloved wife and their child to childbirth. He had wandered aimlessly from odd job to odd job since her death, trying to piece together his life. The loss had left him withdrawn.

With the cash he had saved over the years, he purchased a ninety-six-acre plot of land that contained a decent four-room house near a small stream. He had a plow, two crosscut saws, hand tools and a bed. He hoped the cash he had left would carry him through until the farm could provide income.

He worked hard clearing trees and removing rocks to create tillable fields. He acquired a reputation with the folks in the area as being a very hard worker. From sunup to sundown, seven days a week, he worked the land. After two years, the farm started to take shape. And, in time, he met and began to court Anna Lambeth, the granddaughter of Samuel Lambeth, one of the first settlers in the area. They married, and in the spring of 1845 Anna gave birth to a strapping young boy, Lucas.

As he sat on a section of log that was waiting to be split, Luke considered what was coming. He tried to see things the way his father would. He knew his father's first wife and child had died a long time ago, but his father never spoke of them to him. Maybe he did to his mother, Anna, but he never talked to Luke about his past.

Luke's dog, Jeff — the one animal he cared about — came over and put his head on his lap, as if he sensed Luke's sadness.

Luke also thought about the farm. The soil was not a rich loam. It had turned out to be thin, with few natural nutrients to grow crops. The soil was shallow, with more and more rocks appearing each year. It was as if the rocks grew during the winters and blossomed in the spring. He wasn't certain, but he suspected that the farm's income was causing a problem. While they had enough to eat, money seemed to be a continuous topic of conversation between his parents.

The farm was home to Luke. It was all he knew, and he loved his life. He tried to do whatever he was asked and, with only a couple of exceptions, he felt his parents were pleased. Every day was different with the kinds of experiences only a farm boy could appreciate. He was happy. He just wanted his life to continue as it was.

Inside the house, Jonas was trying to cool down and figure out what he had to do. He did not want to confront his son when he was angry. He had to give it some thought. On the one hand, the boy was just being a boy, enjoying the horse. His intentions were probably innocent, but he had clearly used poor judgment. On the other hand, he was another mouth to feed, and the farm was providing only the barest profit. He had discussed this situation with Anna, but she could not see or understand the problem. The land was becoming infertile, and either they would have to change from a crop farm to pure livestock, or they would have to move. Jonas, who was now in his late fifties, preferred the latter. But to move and start all over again would be very difficult at his age.

The continuing rift between the Northern and Southern states was an ongoing discussion between Jonas, Anna and to a lesser degree, Luke. Some of their neighbors were strong abolitionists and some very much believed it was all about states' rights. Jonas and Anna deeply resented the radicals from both sides for stirring up so much trouble.

During the past year, most of their neighbors' sons had signed up for Confederate service and Luke felt left out. Many of his best friends had joined up weeks and months ago, and he felt conspicuous, sensing that people might suspect he lacked patriotism, or even worse, was a coward. Luke knew the South had a much stronger cavalry and better riders than the North, and he preferred to become a cavalryman. He had heard of men like Nathan Bedford Forrest, and their swashbuckling daring naturally appealed to Luke.

When Jonas walked into the woodshed, his face was still red and tense, his lips were pinched, and dark bags hung down from his eyes. His jaw was set so hard the facial muscles contorted his appearance. He sat down on an old stool across from Luke and just stared down on the dirt floor for several moments. Finally Jonas looked up with a bereaved sadness.

"Luke, as you probably know, trying to eke out a living on our farm is becoming increasingly difficult. Each year we have had to draw from our now depleted savings just to buy seed for our next crops. We do not make enough to cover what it costs us, and I fear we have to make some changes if your mother and I are to make it through these times. Your reckless behavior this morning," he continued, "has made our situation worse. We will probably have to put the mare down and we cannot afford to replace her."

"But Pa," Luke interjected, "she might be okay."

"Let me finish, Luke. What I am trying to tell you is while your mother and I dearly love you, you are not contributing to this homestead. We have talked about this before…about some of the reckless things you do. Again and again, you act immaturely and put your mother and me at risk. You need to move on, Luke. Maybe when you grow up and become a man, you will come back and we'll work together to make this a respectable farm. But until that happens, you are of no practical use to us. Who knows, maybe a couple of years in the army might just put some sense into that head of yours." Jonas just sat on the old stool, looking down as if he had said all he was going to say.

Luke stared at his father, his mouth open. He was unable to speak. His mind was flooded with emotions. Rejection, sadness, anger, rebellion, all hit him at once. Grasping the gravity of what his father had just said, he let tears flow freely down his cheeks. For a long time, neither said a word. At length, Luke stood up and started walking toward the door. As he did so, he said, "I'll be gone before morning."

Jonas looked down at the dirt floor with his teeth still clenched, not moving.

The sun was high in the sky as Luke started walking toward town. He had not wanted to confront his mother, and walking out seemed the easiest thing to do.

As he passed the local post office, he stopped and looked at both sides of the front door. On the right was a bright new enlistment poster for the Confederate States of America and on the left was an old poster for the Union that had been mutilated and smeared with mud. He studied one, then the other, over and over.

The Union poster said something about saving the Union, while the Confederate poster brightly headlined, "Wanted: 100 Good Men To Repel Invasion." Luke thought about the messages. Yes, it did seem like an invasion, he concluded. What right does the North have coming down here and trying to force us to stay in the Union? Remembering the phrase "independent states…" in the Declaration of Independence, any doubt he had about who was right and who was wrong went away and his mind was made up.

When he walked through the front door, the postmaster recognized him. "Hi, Luke," he said. "No mail for the Pettigrews today." He looked at Luke more closely, noticing his slumped shoulders and red eyes. Luke's shirt had stains from his fall off the horse and was torn at the elbow. His face was covered with dust and dried streaks from his tears. His curly light brown hair was disheveled and caked with dirt. "What's wrong, son? You look like you came out on the bad end of a fight with a polecat."

"Fell off the horse," was all Luke could manage. "How would I go about enlisting?"

The postmaster replied, "The Tennessee 28th is camped just west and a little south of here, and the sergeant is due here in a couple of hours. He's always looking for recruits. We have quite a few boys from here in the 28th, and they're all itching to get a chance to push the Yankees back north where they belong."

Luke sat down on a stool next to an iron stove. He put his head down and covered his face with his hands. His head was reeling from his father's words, "You need to move on…" His stomach started to churn and he felt nausea creeping in. He got up suddenly, walked out to the side of the front porch and vomited. He sat on the bench looking down on the weathered wooden floor, not seeing. He was numb, forlorn, rejected, alone.

As Luke sat, staring blindly, he remembered more of what his father had said, "Maybe when you grow up and become a man, you can come back…" He felt his face turn red and the hurt gave way to anger. "I'll show him," he thought, "I'll go off to this goddamn war. I'll be somebody. I'll do some daring deed, save lives, be a big hero. He will live to regret what he said. I'll prove him wrong, and he'll beg me to come back. Maybe I won't come back even if he asks me. I'll prove him wrong! He will be proud of me and will regret what he said."

Slowly, a sense of determination came over Luke. He'd wait for the sergeant from the Tennessee 28th to arrive.

Made in the USA
San Bernardino, CA
30 August 2016